D1015518

GROWING PAINS

GROWING PAINS

Adapted From the Hit TV Series
by N. H. Kleinbaum

Bantam Books, Inc.

ISBN 0-553-26881-3

GROWING PAINS

Chapter 1

"Mom! Dad! You won't believe this! We have a speck-led chickadee out by the garage! Hurry! Come look before it flies away!"

Maggie and Jason Seaver looked questioningly at one another across the kitchen table. "So?" they asked in unison, eyeing their fifteen-year-old son, Mike, skeptically.

Mike bolted from the window to the table. He pushed a thick book on bird life under his mother's nose. "This is important!" he said, pointing to a picture in the book. "Don't you realize that the speckled chickadee is almost exclusively indigenous to the lower Adirondack Valley? And here we are on Long Island, in southern New York, and we've got a freak of nature outside!" Mike dashed back to the window, not even noticing the quizzical glances his family exchanged.

"We've got a freak of nature in here, too," nine-year-old Ben commented as he spooned thick glogs of chocolate sauce over his ice cream.

1

"Maybe two," thirteen-year-old Carol said, eyeing Ben's concoction.

Maggie watched Mike at the window squinting his eyes and peering intently outdoors. She walked over to him. "Gee, Mike," she said suspiciously, "I didn't realize you were such a woodsy kind of guy!"

"Mike turned toward her, an expression of shock on his face. "Me? Heck yeah! I mean, Mom, sometimes I feel more at home outdoors than I do in my own bedroom," he replied.

Ben and Carol stifled their laughter.

"That's because outdoors is cleaner than your room, Mike," his father said. He walked to the window and glanced out for a peek at this supposed incredible bird. "Indoors you're a slob."

"I'm serious, Dad." A crushed look crossed Mike's face. "For me, nature's always been a great release from the pressures of suburban life."

"This could only involve a trip, lessons, or a girl," his father interrupted. "And so, what you really mean is that you want . . ."

"Oh, Dad, really!" Mike said. "Well, actually," he added, "I do want to go camping this weekend with Jimmy and Boner and Boner's older brother, Mitch. Mitch is the most mature kid in the whole school," Mike begged.

"He ought to be." Carol snickered as she poured a thin stream of raspberry sauce over her ice cream. "He's twenty-one!"

"Eighteen, twenty-one, what's the difference?" Mike shot back. "He's a mature guy. What do you say, Mom, can I go, please?"

Maggie looked at her sandy-haired son and wrinkled her forehead in doubt. "So, Mike, what do you and your friends plan to do all weekend?'' she asked.

Mike put his arm around his mother's shoulders and squeezed her warmly. He closed his eyes and said dramatically, ''To breathe free, Mom. Breathe free!''

''And once you've got the hang of that?'' his father asked. ''What happens then?''

Mike smiled innocently, looking from his mother to his father. ''Then? . . . Oh, the usual . . . a little fishing, hiking.'' He lowered his voice and quickly mumbled, ''Dirt-biking,'' then continued in his normal voice, ''bird-watching, and stuff like that.''

Maggie turned away from the window. ''Wait a minute, wait a minute,'' she said. ''What was that before bird-watching?''

Imitating Mike's mumbling, Ben repeated, ''Dirt-biking, you know Mom, dirt-biking!''

''Okay! Okay!'' Mike shouted, flashing an angry glance at his little brother. Ben always seemed either to get him in trouble or else to demand a payoff to keep him out of trouble. ''Dirt-biking. I said, 'dirt-biking.' Okay?''

Maggie glared at Mike and then turned to her husband. ''Jason, may I have a word with you in the living room?'' she mumbled, imitating Mike.

''What?'' Jason looked up questioningly.

''The living room!'' she said sternly.

''You know, Dad. She said the 'living room,' '' Ben mimicked, covering his mouth to hide a broad grin. ''What's wrong with you people?''

Mike glared at Ben as Maggie grabbed Jason's arm and pulled him into the hall.

''We may have switched roles recently,'' Maggie said, slamming the living room door shut and turning to face Jason, ''but we can still talk like equal parents. So what do you have to say about your son's latest request?'' she asked, flopping onto the couch.

Jason sat in a nearby chair. ''Well, he's your son, too!'' he answered.

''But since you're the one who's home with the kids now, I'm sure this request comes because of your influence,'' Maggie growled. ''You know how much you talk about your old Harley motorcycle days!''

''Great days,'' Jason mused.

''Enough daydreaming, Jason,'' Maggie said. ''We have to work out the kinks in our new arrangement. Just because I'm back at the newspaper and you're seeing patients at home doesn't mean I don't want a voice in what happens here!''

''Maggie, with your persistence, no one, not even I, could take your voice away,'' Jason chided. ''Listen, it takes a while to work out this role-reversal stuff. Personally, I love it. You've never looked greater. You obviously love reporting. And after fifteen years on the frontline being home with the kids, you deserve a chance to work at your profession.''

Tears welled up in Maggie's eyes. ''Oh, Jason, that's so sweet,'' she cried, putting her arms around his neck. ''I feel so guilty some mornings, running out to the newspaper. And then, if I'm covering a meeting or doing an interview, the kids might not even be able to reach me. I never had to worry about leaving the kids before.''

''Listen,'' Jason said, putting his hands on her shoulders, ''you're here whether you're in the house or not! And the kids are proud of you. They love to see your byline in the paper. Did you hear Ben telling Timmy that his Mom had lunch with a movie star the other day? They're proud of you—and so am I.''

"But after all those years of your working in the hospital is it fair to have you be home now?" she asked.

"I love it! It's a change for me, too." Jason smiled. "No cafeteria lunches. No sterile conference rooms. The patients come here, and all is fine. And look, if this role reversal doesn't work out for either of us, we'll talk it over. We can make changes so it does work."

Maggie sniffled. Jason handed her a handkerchief.

"I guess you're right," she said, blowing her nose loudly. "I do want to do something for me, but I don't want to hurt you or the kids in the process," she admitted.

"Listen, right now we have to solve this dirt-biking business, and I think Mike shouldn't go," Jason said. "With no experience, he could really hurt himself."

"I agree," Maggie said. "I think it's important that we present a unified front to the kids, and I'm definitely opposed to dirt-biking."

Mike stood anxiously outside the living room. Even with his ear pressed against the door, he couldn't make anything out of the muffled sounds within. He turned to Ben and Carol, who were standing in the kitchen doorway watching his discomfort with mild amusement.

"I wish I knew what they were saying," Mike said, moving back into the kitchen."

"I know what they're saying," Carol said. She struck a pose her mother took in these kinds of situations. " 'We've got to present a unified front to the kids, Jason,' " she imitated.

"Hey, that was pretty good, Carol," Ben piped in. "And Dad is saying, 'Come on, Maggie, I know Mike's screwed up before. But we can't raise the kid in a bubble!' "

Carol interrupted, "And Mom is saying, 'I don't see why not. It's not as if it's never been done!' "

Ben laughed and said, "Now Dad is saying, 'Maggie, you're overreacting!' "

Mike grimaced as his brother and sister howled with laughter. "It's not funny, you guys! My life, my reputation as a cool guy is on the line here. You don't know anything!"

In the living room, Maggie and Jason continued their conversation.

"I'm not overreacting!" she said. "I just don't want to see him get himself killed up there."

Jason rose from his chair and sat on the couch next to Maggie. "Honey," he said, "he could get killed right here. He could fall down the stairs; he could drown in the tub." Jason stopped speaking and looked thoughtful for a moment. "He could choke on my pastrami surprise!"

Maggie jumped up and stamped her feet. "Well, that does it," she said, walking toward the door. "Tomorrow we're going to get that kid a bubble!"

"How can you eat ice cream at a time like this?" Mike asked Carol, who sat calmly at the kitchen table while Mike paced back and forth waiting for his parents to return.

Carol methodically worked her spoon around the dish of ice cream. "Don't you have studying to do, anyhow?" she asked, pausing with her spoon in midair. "I heard that Mr. DeWitt is giving a killer of a history midterm. Everyone I know in your class is starting to study for it now. How can you go camping at a time like this?"

"Don't worry about it, Carol." Mike grimaced, dismissing the suggestion. "History is not the issue now. Camping is."

Carol shook her head. "I don't see how you do so little homework. I always have homework. This weekend I have this big paper to do on dreams, and all you're worried about is camping with those dumb friends of yours."

The suspense of waiting for his parents to return was getting to Mike. He didn't even respond to Carol's crack about his friends. "Come on, who's kidding who?" Mike almost shouted at Carol and Ben. "They won't make me stay home because of DeWitt's test. They'll make me stay home because camping's FUN!"

"It won't be fun if you flunk your midterm," Carol pressed.

"Get real, Carol," Mike snapped. "Just drop it! One brain in this family is enough. You worry about tests. I want to go camping!"

The door swung open, and Maggie and Jason walked into the kitchen. "Okay, Mike," his mother said, reluctantly. "You can go camping. But no dirt-biking."

Mike's mouth dropped open. "No dirt-bi—?"

"That's it," his father said. "Take it or leave it. Camping is in. Dirt-biking is out!"

Mike gulped and sighed. "Okay," he said with a shrug. "Thanks."

Mike sat on a log beside the campfire reading a sexy girlie magazine out loud to Boner and Jimmy. " 'I want you, Joanne. I need you because I am a man.' " He snorted. " 'And so, at last, finally, I mean now, I get to realize my dream.' "

Pretending to be "Joanne," Boner asked in a high-pitched voice, " 'What is your dream?' "

Mike turned the page, anxious to continue. His mouth dropped open. "Do you believe this? Do you believe this?" he asked incredulously. " 'To be continued in next month's issue!' Oh, great!" Shaking the magazine, Mike threw it into the fire. "What junk," he said. "This thing doesn't even have a centerfold."

"Way to go, Boner," Jimmy chided as he punched the scruffy-looking boy beside him. "You brought us great entertainment."

The punching stopped at the sound of a dirt-bike engine.

"Here comes Mitch," Boner said, pointing to his older brother, who was sailing across the hill toward the campsite.

Slamming to a halt in front of the trio, Mitch hopped off the bike and turned to Mike. "You're up, Seaver," the grungy-looking, heavier version of Boner, grunted.

"Ah, look, Mitch, I told you. I dirt-biked my brains out last summer and I'm kind of burned out on the experience."

"Wait a minute, Seaver," Boner interrupted. "Didn't you tell me last week that you'd never tried one of these?"

"Yeah," Mike agreed, pointing to the dirt bike. "One of THESE. I mean, this, the Oshima seven-oh-five. Now, I've tried the seven-oh-two, the seven-oh-three, seven-oh-four, and almost everything else. I just meant one of THESE!"

"Oshima don't make no seven-oh-four, Seaver," Mitch growled as he moved toward Mike.

"Yeah," Mike said. He walked over to the bike and ran his hands along the handlebars. "Because when I tested the prototype, I told 'em it was a piece of garbage!"

"You're not afraid of the seven-oh-five, are you, Mikey?" Mitch teased, giving Mike a push.

"Hey, look, you guys," Mike said, taking a deep breath. "I'm just not supposed to."

Boner, Jimmy, and Mitch stared at Mike, then burst into laughter. "Who says?" Boner asked. "Your mommy?"

"No, not my mommy. Ha! My mommy! The jokes

just don't stop coming with you guys, do they?" He laughed, trying to disguise his uneasiness. "Well, see, the fact is that, well, several prominent doctors have advised that breaking any more bones could kind of ruin my chances of turning pro."

"I didn't know they had professional wusses," Mitch jabbed and broke into hysterical laughter. Mike's friends joined in.

"Hey," Mike shouted, looking trapped. "I'm not a wuss, okay?"

"No, no, no, he's not a wuss. He just does a good imitation of one." Mitch howled again.

"Hey, knock it off," Mike yelled as the other three continued to laugh at him.

Mitch, Boner, and Jimmy looked at each other, suddenly silent. "OOOO-ooooh," they teased in unison. "Mikey's mad!"

Mike grabbed the dirt bike. "Give me the bike! Just give me the bike!" he shouted as he climbed awkwardly on the seat. "But I'm not doing any stunts," he added. He started the engine and revved it up noisily. After a moment's hesitation, the bike bolted, and Mike headed up the hill.

The three boys watched Mike and the bike fly off into the distance. "Whew! Look at him go!" Boner whistled. Their heads bobbed up and down in unison as Mike flew across the hilly terrain.

"Wow!" Boner said. "I didn't realize those things could go through a bush like that!"

"Holy Toledo," Mitch yelled. "Now he's got his elbows wrapped around the handlebars!" Mitch began running toward the hill. Boner and Jimmy followed. "Look!" Mitch called. "He's hanging from the tail pipe!"

Boner raised his hand above his eyes and peered after

the roaring dirt bike. "And he said he wasn't gonna do any stunts!"

The three watched the bike zigzag across the rough hillside. Suddenly, there was a loud crash.

"Holy cow!" Mitch cried as the dirt bike rolled down the hill toward them. As it came closer, they realized there was no rider. "What happened to Seaver?" Mitch yelled. They all looked toward the bush. Then they looked down at the empty bike in silence. Seconds later, Mitch, Boner, and Jimmy took off up the hill. They arrived in time to see Mike trying to pull himself out of a bush.

"Hey, guys," Mike called, forcing a cheerful smile. "Great run, huh? Did you see some of those loop-the-loops? I told you I'm a pro at this stuff!"

Boner looked down at Mike, who was covered with dirt, blood, and bruises. "You mean, you expect us to believe you did that on purpose?" he asked.

Mike looked up in surprise. He forced himself to hide the scorching pain in his arms and his seat. "Of course I do. You're my friends. You're not all that bright, but you're still my friends."

Mitch reached out and helped Mike to his feet. "Whoa," he called out, pointing. "Look at the back of his pants!"

"What's wrong with the back of my pants?" Mike asked.

"They're not there!" Mitch answered.

"We'd better go home and get you to a doctor," Jimmy said. "This looks bad."

Mike dusted himself off and tried to walk. "No, no, man, look, I'm fine, fine. Really. I just need to sit down a minute."

Mitch and Jimmy helped him over to a nearby log.

Mike bent to sit on the log, and his face instantly contorted with pain. He jumped back to his feet. "Ha-ha-ha-ha." He forced a laugh. "Maybe I did get a little scraped up."

With Mike hobbling, he and his friends headed down the hill to Mitch's pickup truck. "You wait in the cab while we load up the stuff," Mitch ordered Mike.

"Listen, guys, I'll be okay. Really."

"Seaver, if you ride, you ride right. If you get hurt, you see a doctor," Mitch barked. "Now get in the cab and we'll get you to a doctor."

Mike nodded in silent agreement and climbed carefully into the front seat, trying to keep from actually sitting. Boner and Jimmy gathered up the camping gear, and Mitch loaded the dirt bike into the back. Then he climbed into the cab, and Boner and Jimmy hopped in the back with the equipment.

"Let's go, Seaver," Mitch said, shaking his head. "You idiot."

Mitch drove into town and parked outside the medical group office across from the local hospital. "Go on in and see someone, Seaver," he ordered. "We'll wait for you out here."

"Yeah, sure, Mitch," Mike said, smiling painfully. "See ya."

After a brief interrogation by the receptionist, Mike was led into an examination room. He undressed, put on a paper exam gown, and stood waiting for a doctor.

A pretty nurse, carrying a clipboard, opened the door and entered. "May I have your name again, sir?" she asked, looking suspiciously at Mike.

"Uh, McManus, Bartholomew McManus," Mike answered, using a deep, gruff voice.

"Well, Bartholomew . . ."

"Just call me Barth." Mike smiled.

The nurse chuckled. "Okay, Barth. The doctor will see you in a moment. Why don't you just have a seat on the examination table?"

Mike nodded and instinctively started to sit. He froze as he remembered his condition and straightened up. "No, no," he said, laughing. "I'll stand. I sit all day."

Just then the doctor came into the room. "I'll need Mrs. Cramden's Xrays, Nurse," he said. Then he turned to his patient. "Michael! Michael Seaver!"

"Dr. McCloskey!" Mike said in a panicked voice. "Look, I—I didn't think you worked on weekends! Don't you have a substitute doctor?"

"Oh, you mean Dr. Emmett? He's on vacation this week."

As he hurriedly grabbed his clothes and headed for the door, Mike said, "Well, then you must be very, very busy. Why don't I just come back some other time?"

"Nonsense. Nonsense," Dr. McCloskey said. "Why don't you just jump up here? Now what seems to be the trouble?" He gently pushed Mike down on the examination table.

"Ahhhh!" Mike winced, unable to hide the pain.

"I guess that says it all," Dr. McCloskey observed. "Let's have a look."

Mike leaned over on the examination table, his face contorted with pain. The doctor lifted the paper gown to examine the damage. "Hmmm," he said, sounding concerned.

"It's just a little scratch, Doc," Mike said nonchalantly. "Really, it's nothing."

"That looks bad, Mike," Dr. McCloskey said.

"Seems to be broken in half!"

Mike scowled as the doctor laughed at his own joke.

"Now, seriously," Dr. McCloskey added, tapping Mike on the rear. "Does that hurt?"

"Yeow!!!" Mike yelled.

"Not really, huh?" Dr. McCloskey said nonchalantly. "How did this happen, Mike?"

Mike stood up and looked at Dr. McCloskey. "To tell you the truth, Doc, it's kind of always been like this. It's just acting up."

"Mike!" the doctor said, giving him a serious look.

"Okay, okay. I went to a party and sat on a hot pizza," he said with a straight face.

"Oh, well there seem to be some abrasions," Dr. McCloskey said.

"Those are cheese burns," Mike answered gravely.

"And what about the gravel?"

"Ah, we didn't order that," Mike said sincerely, while the doctor smiled behind his back.

"Okay, Mike. I'll give you some cream to apply to those, ah, pizza burns, and a prescription for some antibiotics, just to be safe. And next time you have a pizza party," he added. "Stay on your feet!"

"Ha-ha-ha-ha." Mike's laugh was hollow. "Yeah, sure."

"I wonder how Mike's doing," Ben mused. He was stretched out on the sofa mulling over a dream he was reciting to Carol for her report.

Carol shuffled through a sheaf of papers on her lap. "What?" she asked absentmindedly. "Mike? Oh, don't worry about that now. Get on with your dream. This is really exciting. I think I'm going to make a breakthrough.

This will be great for my paper!''

"Oh, yeah,'' Ben said, clearing his throat and looking suddenly dreamy-eyed. "My dream. Well, I'm flying over New York in my underwear, and then all of a sudden people start yelling, 'Hey, look, it's inside out!' ''

"Now wait,'' Carol interrupted. "Is this before or after the one where you were 'Ben: The Forgotten Kennedy' ?''

"It was before that,'' Ben said. "And after the one where I turned into the human hot dog.''

Carol wrinkled her brow and looked at Ben suspiciously. "Ben, you know I'm getting graded on this paper. You're not just making this stuff up, are you?''

"Making it up?'' Ben asked with sincere astonishment. "No! Carol, these are REAL dreams!''

"You swear?''

"Cross my heart. I'd never make up a dream.''

"Great.'' Carol picked up her papers and headed for the door. "This should be enough for a penetrating psychological profile of the REAL Ben Seaver. See ya.'' She waved, closing the door as she left.

"Penetrating and profitable.'' Ben said, grinning broadly. He pulled a pile of dollar bills from his pocket and spread them on the table like a deck of cards.

At the sound of a motorcycle engine, Ben stashed the money in his jeans pocket and ran to the window. Outside, his father sat proudly atop a dirt bike, singing, " 'Get your motor runnin' . . . vroom, vrooom, vrooom!' ''

"Wow, look at Dad,'' Ben shouted and ran for the door.

Outside, Jason straddled the dirt bike near the front door. " 'Head out on the highway . . . vroom, vrooom, vrooom,' '' he continued, slightly off-key.

Maggie opened the door and looked at him. "Jason,

what the . . .''

" 'Yes, I'm looking for adventure . . . ooh, babe,' ''
he crooned, spotting Maggie and beaming a mischievous
smile. " 'And whatever comes my way. Woo, woo, wooo
. . .' ''

"Jason, are you crazy?'' Maggie giggled.

"Why? Because I was born wild?'' he asked, steering
the dirt bike into the house.

"No,'' she said, unable to hide a smile. She followed
him inside. "Because you have a dirt bike in my living
room. And,'' she added, looking at the tires, "it's dirty!''

Jason shook his head and shrugged. "Well, we also
have a very unhappy teenage son right now. So I thought,
'Why not go out, rent a dirt bike, and teach him to ride
myself?' That way, he won't ride off his bottom, or
something.''

"What a sweet and incredibly terrifying idea.'' Maggie
grimaced.

"Maggie, I know what I'm doing. I used to ride a
Harley, for crying out loud!''

"I know, sweetheart.'' Maggie smiled. "I visited you
in the hospital. Remember?'' Maggie looked again at the
dirt bike, kissed Jason affectionately, and walked from the
living room, shaking her head.

"Hey!'' Jason called after her. "That cow came out
of nowhere and ran right into my bike! Oh, well,'' he said,
sitting back on the seat. He closed his eyes and began singing
again as his thoughts turned back to his own biking days.

"I'm going to kill you!'' Carol shrieked, interrupting
Jason's biking memories. She stormed into the living room,
chasing a terrified Ben.

"I'm going to kill you back,'' Ben yelled, turning
toward his father for protection. "Nice bike, Dad,'' Ben

said, trying to change the subject. "I was just on my way out to see if I could have a ride when this zombie attacked me," he added, pointing to Carol.

Red-faced and fuming, she screamed, "You can't kill me, you idiot! You'll be dead!"

"Not if I go slowly!" Ben said. They each reached for the other's neck and began choking one another.

Jason hopped off the bike and ran to push them apart. "Whoa, hold on. I'll do the killing around here," he said. "Now, what's going on?"

"Ben ruined my paper!" Carol wailed.

"Not 'Portrait of a Sleeping Nine-Year-Old'?" her father asked.

"Oh, Dad!" Carol slumped onto the couch. "He said all the dreams he sold me were real. I paid him cold cash for those dreams. This thief made a fortune on my paper! And now I catch him out on the front lawn buying a nightmare from Ralph Fensterwald. For twenty-five cents!"

"Hey! I said they were real dreams. I didn't say they were mine!" Ben said innocently.

"Ben, you creep! You thief! You paperwrecker!" Carol shouted.

"So I bought a few off some friends. I barely broke even," he said, shrugging.

"Ben," his father said, his tone serious.

"Okay, okay, so I made a two-hundred-percent profit," he admitted. Carol and Jason stared at him. "Is that such a crime? We live in a free enterprise system, don't we?"

"But you ruined my paper," Carol moaned. "Now all my conclusions are meaningless."

Jason looked from Ben to Carol. "Oh, I don't know, honey," he said. "I think there might still be a paper in this somewhere. Say 'The Emergence of the Criminal Mind,' or 'The Side Effects of Swift and Severe Punishment,' such as, oh, say, Ben's doing your chores for a weekend?''

Ben jumped to his feet. "What?!!!"

Nodding agreement, Carol smiled and turned to her father. "That's a good idea, Dad. But I think it would take a lot more than a weekend to get reliable data. I'd need at least a week," she said triumphantly.

"Sounds like a good idea to me," her father agreed. "What do YOU think, Ben?"

"I hate it." Ben scowled and sat down again.

"Okay, then," his father said cheerfully, "let's make it a month!"

"A week sounds fair," Ben said hastily, accepting defeat.

Jason knelt down dramatically in front of Ben, who sat stewing over his punishment. "Ben! Ben! Ben!" he said, putting his arm around his youngest son. "Never, never, never sell your dreams!"

Nodding his head in agreement, Ben said, "Are you kidding? Not at these prices!"

Mike peeked through the greenhouse window into the kitchen. "All clear," he said to himself. He bit his lip as he slowly opened the door and started to tiptoe across the kitchen floor. Suddenly, his mother turned and slammed the refrigerator door shut. Mike stopped in his tracks, forced a smile, and struck a casual pose.

"Mike?" his mother said in surprise.

"Mom? Have you lost weight?" Mike asked innocently. He leaned against a kitchen chair in pain. "You look terrific today!"

"What are you doing here?" his mother asked.

"Here? Here?" Mike said, looking around. "Mom, um, let me ask you this: What are ANY of us doing here? It's a timeless question. I think a dead philosopher once said . . ."

"Mike!" His father walked into the kitchen. "What are you doing here?"

"Dad! Have you lost weight? You look terrific today!"

Maggie put down the lettuce she was holding and walked cautiously over to Mike. "Mike, how come you're home early?"

Mike shifted on his feet. "Well, to tell you the truth, Mom, I kind of got in a little argument with Boner."

"Ah. Well, I'm sorry to hear that, Mike," his father said. "But I'm glad you're home. Because I have a terrific surprise for you! Come on, big buddy, take a look!" Jason bounced toward the living room and waved Maggie and Mike to follow.

Mike walked very slowly, as though his knees wouldn't bend.

Maggie gave a curious look as she watched Mike's strange walk. "Mike, are you okay?" she asked. "How come you're walking like that?"

"Uh, I'm fine, Mom. I'm just trying to keep the suspense alive here."

As they entered the living room, Mike gasped. Before him, Jason stood proudly pointing to the dirt bike perched in front of the coffee table.

"There she is, Mike!" His father beamed. Mike froze. "Is that a mean machine, or what?" his father asked, looking at Mike expectantly.

"Aaaaagh!" Mike whimpered.

"Look at this baby. This is the Oshima seven-oh-five!

What a beauty," his father said excitedly. "Ever seen one of these babies, Mike?"

"Uh, yeah, once," Mike said. "It was going the other way."

Maggie walked over to Mike and put her arm around his shoulder. She felt him stiffen suddenly. "Your father rented it for the week so he could teach you how to ride," she said. "Wasn't that sweet?"

"Oh, gee, yeah." Mike smiled. "What a dad! What a pal! What a guy! Well," he said suddenly, "I'm off to bed. Didn't sleep much around the campfire last night."

"Bed?" his mother asked in surprise. She was about to say more when the telephone rang. "Oh, no! That's probably my editor. I was supposed to call him back." Maggie moved toward the door. "I'll take it in the kitchen."

"Bed?" his father echoed. "Mike, the bike! C'mon, plant that duff up here." He patted the seat of the dirt bike.

"Which duff? Where?" Mike asked hesitantly.

"Come on, Mike! Get on!" Jason slapped Mike on the rear end with enthusiasm.

"Aaaaaagh!" Mike yelled.

"Hop on!" his father urged. "I'm really excited about this!" He patted the seat lovingly.

Mike carefully climbed on the bike and hovered over the seat without actually touching it. His face contorted with pain. "Ah," he said, swallowing hard. "Comfortable."

"Come on, fella, get into it." Jason shoved Mike down onto the seat. "Sit down! It's not going to bite you!" Jason pounded his hands vigorously up and down on the seat. "It's got great suspension, too, doesn't it, Mike? Nice, huh?"

"Yah! Yah! Yah! Yah!" Mike shrieked, too much in pain to say anything more.

"Maggie," Jason yelled, "I think he likes it!"

Mike sighed deeply, bit his lip, and lifted himself off the seat, his rear end burning with pain. As he moved toward the stairs, Jason pulled him back on the bike and jumped on behind him. He fenced Mike in with his arms. Playfully rocking the bike, Jason pretended they were riding double out on the road. "Vroom . . . vrooom. I can feel the wind in our hair already, Mike," he said, laughing.

"Jason," Maggie called from the kitchen. "Might I have a word with you?"

Jason lowered his arms, and Mike instantly leaped off the bike.

"Yeah, Dad! Have words," Mike said. "Have lots of words! There's nothing that says it quite like words!" He began backing toward the door. As Maggie came into the living room, he disappeared in the direction of the kitchen with a weak smile on his face.

Maggie walked over to Jason who was still sitting on the seat of the bike. "Jason, that was Dr. McCloskey on the phone," she said. "It seems Mike stopped by there today."

Jason looked up from the bike. "Oh? What for?"

"Turns out he had some pretty bad bruises and abrasions on his . . . in his gluteal region!"

"He smashed his butt?" Jason said, surprised. "Well, why didn't he tell us? Oh, wait a minute." He looked down at the bike. "Now, could these be the kind of bruises and abrasions you get by, say, falling off a dirt bike?"

Maggie nodded her head. "I just happen to have asked Dr. McCloskey the same question," she said.

"And he said . . .?"

"It was either that or a very freaky shaving accident!"

Jason climbed slowly off the bike. "Uh-huh." He

stepped into the hall. "Oh, Mike," he called sweetly toward the kitchen.

Mike shuffled slowly through the kitchen door.

"Yeah, Dad?"

"Ready to go biking?"

"Uh, now, Dad?"

"Yeah, yeah. Come on." He pulled Mike into the living room. "We're going to take this puppy over some of the roughest terrain on Long Island." He smiled, hopped onto the seat of the bike, and began bouncing up and down.

"Uh-huh," Maggie piped in. "You know your father was out all day scouting for potholes."

"P-p-p-potholes," Mike stammered.

"Yeah," his mother enthused, keeping up the act. "And if you two were real men you'd do it without shock absorbers!"

Jason jumped off the bike and pulled Mike toward it. "Let's take 'em off, Mike! Whaddaya say?!" he asked, his eyes burning with excitement.

"Ah, no, no, Dad. I don't think we should do this!" Mike protested, pulling back. "I mean, dirt bikes are death machines. People fall off and get hurt."

"No way," his father said, waving off the comment. "Only a bonebrain would fall off." Wheeling the bike to the door, he waved Mike to follow.

Mike broke down, pulling back. "No! Please don't make me go!" he cried.

"But why not?" his mother asked innocently. "You've been begging to go dirt-biking. Here's your big chance!"

"Because I'm a bonebrain, that's why," Mike confessed. "I mean, I fell off one of these up at the campground. I promised I wouldn't ride, but I did. And I got hurt! I mean, you warned me. I didn't listen to you! You were right! You're always right. And personally,'' he said, shaking his finger at his parents, ''I find that annoying. What is it with you people, anyhow?''

''I don't know,'' his mother answered. ''Jason, what is it with us people?''

''We can't help it,'' Jason said with a shrug. ''We're older. We're wiser. We're your parents!''

''I find that annoying, too, sometimes,'' Mike said.

''Then wait until you hear this one,'' his father went on. ''I think we agree that you should spend the next week in your room.''

Mike looked from one parent to the other and asked, ''Can I spend it lying on my face?''

Jason and Maggie stifled grins, shrugged, and said in unison, ''Oh, all right!''

''Thanks,'' Mike said and hobbled toward the stairs.

''Hey, Mike?'' his father called.

Mike turned.

''What really upsets us is not just that you went and rode the dirt bike. It's that you tried to deceive us. I mean, if you get hurt, we need to know.''

Mike thought for a moment. ''Does that mean that if I had told you guys, I wouldn't have been punished?'' he asked.

''No way!'' his parents chimed at once.

Mike shrugged. ''Just checking,'' he said. He winced in pain and continued up the stairs.

Jason and Maggie looked at one another and sighed. ''Kids!'' Maggie said. ''Always a challenge!''

''Mom, Dad,'' Carol called. ''The movie starts at seven forty-five! Hurry up!''

Maggie and Jason raced down the stairs. They were pulling on their jackets when Ben walked in from the kitchen. "Everyone ready?" Maggie asked. "We should make it in plenty of time," she added, looking at her watch. "Where's Mike?"

"Is the great roadrunner going to join us?" Ben asked. "I thought he was grounded!"

"Mike! C'mon, Mike," Jason called from the foot of the stairs. "Let's go!"

"I'm not going!" Mike yelled down from his room.

"Mike," his father called up, "we're doing you a favor letting you go. You should be staying at home, but we're letting you go to the movie. Now get your tail down here and don't make everyone late."

"I don't think you should let him go," Carol said. "He hasn't begun to study for his history midterm. You always bend the rules for him."

"Come on, Carol," her mother said. "He really is suffering physically for this one. We bend the rules for all of you kids once in a while."

"I'm not going!" Mike shouted again. "People will see me!"

"No they won't, Mike. We're going to the drive-in," his father yelled up the stairs. "Come on. It'll take your mind off your problem."

"Mike," Carol called up to him. "I think you should stay home. You'll be able to study for your history test!"

At the mention of the history test, Mike appeared at the top of the stairs. A huge white pillow was stuck down the back of his baggy pants. He waddled down the stairs and slowly moved to the door. "All right, all right," he said. "Give a guy a chance to retain some dignity, would you!" He stomped out the door.

Maggie, Jason, Ben, and Carol burst into laughter at Mike's dramatic exit.

"At least he's going," Maggie chuckled. "Even if he does look like a goose-down pillow!"

Covering their mouths and coughing down their laughter, the other Seavers followed Mike's lead out the door and into the car.

Chapter 2

"Mike's lucky that his problem healed up so fast," Jason said, leafing through the newspaper.

"I was worried that he might get an infection, that he might be laid up for awhile," Maggie agreed. "But in less than two weeks he's back to his old . . . impossible . . . self!"

Jason smiled over at Maggie. "How's the feature story coming?" he asked.

"Pretty good," she said. "It's so exciting to be on a newspaper again. I enjoy reporting more now than I did fifteen years ago in my other life. B.C."

"B.C.?" Jason looked amused.

"B.C.!" Maggie smiled. "Before children!"

"I'm getting used to my 'housefather' job, too," Jason said, leaning back in his chair. "I really like being at home. My patients even prefer to come here for their sessions rather than go to the hospital."

"I imagine it must feel easier to go to a house to talk

25

with a psychiatrist,'' Maggie agreed. "It's kind of like seeing a friend.'' She flipped through her notepad and circled facts and figures as she spoke. "The kids are really great with you home now, too, honey,'' she added. "They seem to be doing their chores and getting along well. I guess our role reversal is working out so far.''

Jason smiled. "So far, so good,'' he agreed. He was about to say something else, when Carol and Ben stormed into the living room.

"She's definitely a Wendy and that's final,'' Carol yelled at her brother.

"Uh-uh. HE's clearly a Sam,'' Ben shouted. "What do you know about plants, anyway! Dad! Will you look at this and tell Carol it's a Sam and not a Wendy!''

Jason put down his newspaper. "Dad,'' Carol said as he walked to where she and Ben stood in front of two small, potted plants, "I think I know my own plant. She's a Wendy and that's final!''

"Carol, I went to medical school, okay? So, I think I can settle this.'' Jason lifted the plant and peered clinically at the underside of the pot. "You're right,'' he said to Carol. "It's a Wendy.''

Maggie looked up from her notes, eyeing the trio in confusion. "What ARE you talking about?'' she asked.

"Oh, well, it's an experiment,'' Carol explained. "I've been talking to Wendy here and giving what's-his-name''—she pointed to the second plant—"the silent treatment to see which one grows faster.''

"And the winner becomes tonight's salad!'' her father said, smiling.

The doorbell rang.

"Oh, Dad!'' Carol protested. "This is science. It's research, not Julia Child! Get the door, Ben.''

Ben walked to the front door, opened it, and quickly shut it. With a look of disgust, he announced, "There's a girl here for Mike."

"Ben!" his mother said. "You didn't just leave her standing outside, did you?"

"She's a girl, Mom. What did you want me to do? Let her in?"

Maggie shook her head, got up from the couch and headed for the front door.

"Ben," his father said, "it sounds like you have some pretty strong feelings about girls."

"No, not really," Ben said, shrugging. "I just don't like them."

"Well, Ben," his mother said as she opened the door, "when a friend comes to the door, you should let them . . . in." She gulped, and her jaw dropped when she spotted the guest. "Why, hello," Maggie said hesitantly. She stared at the girl at the door, a spitting image of the rock star Madonna in one of her more scantily clad moments.

"Like, hi!" the girl answered. "I'm Lisa. Is Mike home?"

Maggie stood momentarily mute, gazing at the cocky and self-confident fifteen-year-old. She regained her composure and forced a smile. "Possibly. Quite possibly. Let me check." She turned from the door with a dazed expression.

"Maggie!" Jason said, pointing to the door.

"Oh, yes," Maggie said, forcing a smile. She pulled the door open wider. "Please, come in, Lisa."

"Thanks."

"Would you like to have a seat? I'm Maggie Seaver, Mike's mother. This is his father, Dr. Seaver, and his brother, Ben, and sister, Carol," she said. "And you are?"

she asked, still dazed by the girl's appearance.

"Lisa. I'm Mike's, like, friend." She followed Maggie into the center of the living room and slinked down into a chair.

Ben stared as she crossed her long, sexy legs. Suddenly he jumped up and bolted from the room.

"You have to forgive him," Jason said, clearing his throat. "He doesn't like girls."

"Well, actually, I, like, don't consider myself a girl," Lisa said with a serious expression. "I consider myself a real woman."

Jason looked at Maggie whose eyes had widened as Lisa spoke.

"And rightly so, I'm sure," Maggie said, shaking her head. "I'll call Mike." She walked to the foot of the stairs. "Mike!" she yelled. "Oh, sorry," she said, turning immediately toward Lisa. "He doesn't seem to be home right now."

"Yeah, Mom?" Mike called out at the same instant, coming to the top of the stairs. He was wearing sloppy jeans, a Mickey Mouse T-shirt, and a baseball cap turned backward. He came down a few steps quickly, then spotted Lisa. "Oh!" he said, with surprise. He turned and sprinted back up the stairs and into his room.

"Guess he doesn't like girls, either," Jason said, laughing as Mike disappeared.

"We'll see about THAT!" Lisa said mischievously.

"Ah, yes," Jason said. He cleared his throat again. "So, Lisa, have some dip?" He offered her a plate of guacamole and nachos. "No, huh?" he said when Lisa looked at the plate with disdain.

"Oh, look." Maggie laughed nervously, pointing to the top of the stairs. "Here's Mike! . . . I think."

Mike walked down the stairs slowly. Now he was wearing tight blue jeans and a leather vest, halfway unzipped, with no shirt underneath. Adjusting his sunglasses and chewing on a toothpick, Mike walked into the living room.

"Hey, Lisa, babe. What a pleasant surprise," he oozed casually.

Lisa stared at him. "Well, I was just in the neighborhood," she said with a coy smile. "I was breaking up with my old boyfriend."

"Oh, yeah?" Mike said cheerfully.

"Yeah. He was just too immature." Lisa twirled her hair with her fingers and seductively moistened her lips with her tongue. She continued to stare at Mike.

"Oh," Maggie interrupted, "was he younger than you, Lisa?"

"Younger? No, he was twenty-seven," she said to Maggie, who gulped uncontrollably.

"What an amazing coincidence," Mike said. "Because I was just upstairs on the phone breaking up with my old girlfriend."

Maggie, Jason, and Carol looked at each other, eyebrows raised.

"She was forty-three," Mike said matter-of-factly.

"Yeah, in dog years, maybe," Carol said, laughing. Mike shot her a menacing glance.

"Ah . . . you guys haven't seen Uncle Stan in a while," Mike said to his family. He pointed toward the door. "Why don't you take a walk by his place?"

Jason made a face. "Mike, your Uncle Stan is in Connecticut."

"So?"

"And he's dead," his father added.

"Why don't you guys go have a snack," Mike persisted. He motioned toward the kitchen with his head.

"Right, a snack," Mike persisted. he motioned toward the kitchen with his head.

"Right, a snack," his father repeated. "I am a little hungry, come to think of it. All right. Come on ladies." He rose and herded Carol and Maggie toward the door. "Lisa, very nice to meet you," he called back as he gave Carol a shove.

"You, too, Dr. Seaver. See ya, Maggie. You don't mind if I call you Maggie, do you?" she asked.

Maggie stared past Jason at Mike and the wild creature beside him and shuddered. "Naw," she said, waving off the question. Pulling Carol along with her, Maggie shoved open the living room door.

"Ouch!" Ben cried and held his nose in pain. "You could have broken my face!"

"Well, who told you to peep through the door?" Carol said. "We didn't know we'd be knocking you down."

In the kitchen, Jason, Maggie, and Carol sat down at the table. Ben joined them quickly, holding an ice pack to his aching nose.

"Dad, do you believe the top that girl was wearing?" Carol asked. "She obviously thinks she's some sexy, hot, rock star. You could see right through the . . ."

"Huh?" her father said. "I, uh, didn't notice . . ."

"Aw, come on, Dad. She might as well have had no shirt on at all!"

"Yeah, well, all things considered," he father said, biting his lip. "I'm glad she didn't choose to go that route."

"Me, too." Ben's voice was muffled by the ice pack.

"Carol, why don't you take Ben and go outside," her mother said insistently. "It'll be good for his nose."

"Why?" Carol asked.

"Because I need to talk to your father."

"About Mike's friend with the major-league yabos?" Carol snickered, straightening her back and sticking out her own, less than major, chest. Ben muffled a laugh, and Maggie's temper flared.

"Out!" she yelled. "Both of you! And, Carol, . . . slouch!"

Carol and Ben walked to the door laughing. "Well, what are we supposed to do outside?" Carol asked.

"I don't care!" Maggie spurted angrily. "Talk to the lawn or something."

"No! Don't do that!" Jason yelled after them. "It needs mowing as it is!"

Peering through the back window to make sure Carol and Ben were out of earshot, Jason turned to Maggie. "Did you see the top that girl was wearing?" he said appreciatively.

Maggie made a face. "Jason, she's a tramp!"

"Oh, come on, Maggie. No! I mean, I admit she doesn't dress with a lot of . . ."

"Clothing," Maggie ended the sentence for him.

"Taste," Jason suggested. "But we don't know anything about the girl."

"Jason, she was going out with a twenty-seven-year-old man!"

"Oh, and that makes her a tramp? Well, maybe they shared the same interests."

"THAT makes her a tramp!" Maggie declared.

"Maggie . . ."

"Look, Jason," Maggie said, softening a bit. "She doesn't even giggle the way a fifteen-year-old girl is supposed to giggle."

Jason considered her comment. "Sounds like I'd better call the National Guard." he laughed.

"You know what I mean," Maggie said. "When a fifteen-year-old girl comes to my door asking for my son, SHE should feel awkward. With this girl, *I* feel awkward and uncomfortable!"

At that moment, Mike pushed open the door to the kitchen and entered with Lisa wrapped playfully around his neck, giggling madly.

"See," Jason began, turning to Maggie, "she giggles."

"My mistake," Maggie said through clenched teeth.

"So," Mike said. His voice had a hopeful tone. "Do you think you guys could, uh, leave?"

"Why?" his mother asked.

"So we can have some juice," Mike said.

"You mean, you can't have juice with us in the room?" his father asked in astonishment.

Mike shrugged. He took a carton of juice from the refrigerator and started to fill two glasses. "Fine, fine," he relented. "But I don't know why you bought a house with nine rooms if you're not going to use them."

"Subtle, Mike." Jason smiled. "Very subtle." He pulled Maggie by the arm away from the table and over to the dishwasher. They started to unload it, taking occasional peeks at Mike and Lisa, who were deep in conversation at the table.

"So, anyway," Lisa said to Mike, continuing where she had left off in the living room, "when I told Ed I was breaking up with him, he, like, cried. It was so pathetic."

"Yeah, that is pathetic," Mike agreed. "I, like, never cry."

"Really?" Lisa said with admiration.

"Well, once when a car rode over my foot, I winced a little," Mike admitted. "But that's about it."

"You're so cute, Mike." Lisa giggled, pushing him playfully.

"Hey, what can I say?" Mike smiled in agreement. "Yeah, I'm, like, cute. I'm really cute!"

Maggie grabbed a plate noisily from the dishwasher, rolled her eyes at Jason, and slammed the door of the machine shut.

"Plus," Lisa chirped, "Ed was, like, superpossessive. I mean, he, like, got upset because I went camping with Phil Creawly who's, like, just a friend, basically."

"Basically?" Maggie asked incredulously.

"Mom!" Mike said, raising his eyebrows.

"I'm sorry," his mother said, coming back, to the table and sitting down. "Lisa, how did your parents feel about you going out with a twenty-seven-year-old?" she asked.

"Oh, like, my mother, she was really bummed out," Lisa said, nodding her head.

"Really?" Maggie's voice was hopeful.

"Yeah," Lisa said. "I think *she* wanted to go out with him."

Maggie's face fell, and she shot an I-told-you-so glance toward Jason. "Well, I take it your parents are no longer together then," she said.

"What makes you say that?" Lisa looked surprised.

"Nothing," Maggie said, sighing deeply. "Never mind."

Lisa turned her attention back to Mike. "So, like, anyway, Mike, you wanna do something tonight?"

Mike popped up from his chair, then suddenly took an ultracool attitude at the offer. "Oh, well, I did just end a very special relationship. But I think I've moped around about that long enough," he said.

"Uh, Mike," his mother interrupted. "Don't forget that your father and I are going out with the Koosmans tonight, and you have to stay at home with Ben and Carol."

"Can't we get a sitter?" Mike asked frantically.

Jason shook his head. "On this short notice we'd never find one without an ax."

"So what?" Mike said, panicked. "Ben and Carol are quick on their feet."

"Now, Mike," his father said.

"Okay, okay," Mike agreed with disgust.

"Hey, Mike," Lisa said. "Maybe I could come over here tonight."

"Yeah! That'd be . . ."

"Probably a very boring way for Lisa to spend a Saturday night," Maggie said pointedly.

Mike glared at his mother.

"Oh, no," Lisa said. "It wouldn't be boring, Maggie. I just LOVE to baby-sit!"

"What a woman, huh, Mom?" Mike beamed. "Then it's all set!"

"You betcha," Maggie said, and slumped in her chair.

"Okay, Lisa," Mike said, leading her out of the kitchen and into the living room. "Then I'll see you right here at eight P.M."

Ben came into the living room and flicked on the light. Looking around to make sure he was alone, he walked directly to Carol's two plants. "You are the ugliest plant alive!" he said to the plant Carol called Wendy. "Carol told me privately that she hates you." He chuckled and flashed a devilish grin. Then he froze. A leaf had suddenly dropped from the plant he was insulting. He unfroze a second later when Maggie walked into the living room. Quickly he picked up the leaf and guiltily shoved it in his pocket.

"What are you doing, Ben?" his mother asked.

"Oh, nothing, Mom," he said casually, moving toward the stairs. He raced up them, bumping into Jason who was heading down into the living room.

Maggie looked at Jason nervously. "Okay, all set?" he asked. "Ready for an exciting night at the movies with the Koosmans?"

"Yeah, I guess so," Maggie said. "So, did you talk to him?"

"Yeah."

"Well, what did you say?"

"Well, pretty much what you and I discussed," Jason reported.

"Like what, specifically?" Maggie pressed.

"Well, you know, it was a father-son talk," Jason said, waving his hands in the air.

"Uh-huh," Maggie said, nodding her head. "Forgive me, Jason, I've never had one of those father-son talks. What did you say?"

Jason coughed. "Well, that's where I say, uh, 'How are you doing, son?' And then he says, 'Pretty good, Dad.' Then I say, 'Is that mousse in your hair or is it wet from the shower?' "

"Come on, Jason," Maggie said impatiently. "Get on to the good part."

Jason sat on the couch. "Honey, I just told him that, in general, I think it's better to start slowly with a relationship, to get to know somebody, to get a . . ."

"A medical report!" Maggie finished, squirming.

"That, too," Jason said.

"So, well, what do you think they'll do tonight?" Maggie asked.

"Well, they'll probably . . . watch TV," Jason mused.

"Uh, Jason, what if they, uh"—she hesitated—"don't watch TV?" she added meaningfully.

"Well," Jason said gently, "if two teenage kids want to get together and 'not watch TV,' they're going to find a way to do it!"

"I'm tired." Maggie sighed. "Let's stay home."

"Now, Maggie . . ."

"I want to watch *The Love Boat,* or *The Honeymooners,*" she insisted.

"Bob and Ellen are picking us up in three minutes," Jason said, looking at his watch.

Maggie stared into space. "Are you sure we shouldn't stay home?"

Jason took Maggie's hand. "You know," he said, "What you have to remember is that no matter where we are, there's always this little voice inside Mike's head, saying, 'Mike! This is your mother speaking!' And that's when Mike says, 'Ma, what are you doing here?' And the little voice says, 'I just want to remind you that I love you and I'll always love you even if you break my heart by touching that girl,' " Jason said, imitating Maggie's voice.

"Okay, okay," Maggie said, laughing at the scenario. "So you're saying I've already saddled him with enough guilt to cripple him for life?"

"No, no," Jason said. "I'm just saying that he knows our values, and he knows that we care about him—and I know that he'll consider that anytime he makes one of life's big decisions."

"I hope you're right," Maggie said as the doorbell rang.

As Jason walked to answer the door, Mike came tearing down the stairs. He raced past Maggie and Jason, stopped in front of the door, tousled his hair, and took a deep breath. Casually, he opened the door. Lisa stood there, wearing a revealing white dress. Mike sucked in his breath and looked Lisa over from head to toe. "Come in, come in." He smiled broadly. "Mom, Dad, you remember Lisa?"

Maggie and Jason looked at Lisa and nodded uncertainly.

"Like, hi, sure." Lisa smiled as Mike took her hand.

"They were just leaving," Mike said, pushing his parents out the door. "So have a good time, you two." He beamed. "Give my best to the Koosmans." Quickly he closed the door.

Jason and Maggie stood on the front porch in silence. A car pulled into the driveway and the driver tooted the horn. Jason waved.

"Jason, we are not leaving the house!" Maggie hissed.

"Maggie," Jason urged, "the Koosmans are here!" He smiled and waved again at the car. "Let's just go!"

"The heck with the Koosmans," Maggie said in a low voice, smiling brightly toward the car but refusing to budge.

"Come on, guys, let's go," Bob Koosman called to Maggie and Jason, standing frozen on the porch.

"Do you want to go and tell Bob and Ellen that we can't leave our house because there's a girl in it?" Jason whispered.

"Why not?" Maggie said, her voice rising. "Would you leave Carol in there with a boy who looked like he just fell off an X-rated wedding cake?! That's a double standard!"

"Nobody said life was fair," Bob Koosman called from the car, having overheard Maggie. "Come on, Maggie. Let's go!''

Jason put his arms on Maggie's shoulders. "Honey, I know what you're feeling, but we shouldn't try to make this decision for Mike. No matter what happens, he's going to live through it.''

"That's comforting," Maggie said, looking back toward the house as she let Jason lead her down the stairs.

"Hey," Bob Koosman said. "I saw her walk up! At least he'll die happy!''

"I hate Bob Koosman," Maggie growled softly as she and Jason walked toward the car.

"Come on, Maggie," Bob Koosman said, poking her arm as they sat in the movie theater. "Have some junk food." He offered her a bucket of popcorn and a box of Raisinettes. "It'll take your mind off your Casanova son and his sexy girlfriend.''

"No, thanks, Bob," Maggie said icily. The lights dimmed and the movie screen flickered to life. Maggie turned her attention to the screen. She stiffened apprehensively as she watched the drama unfold.

"Hold me, Ralph," the female character on the screen said, as hot, romantic music filled the theater.

"Do you know how long I've waited for this?" Ralph asked. "For the opportunity to do this? This is an incredible opportunity for me to do what I've always . . .''

"Shut up and hold me!" the woman's voice insisted.

". . . you have so many places to hold!" Ralph said.

"Just shut up and pick one!" the female character cried.

Jason was turning his head to various angles trying to stay with the action that it heated up on the screen.

Maggie watched for several moments. Then, horrified,

she jumped out of her seat and started to leave. Jason grabbed her arm and pulled her back onto her seat. "This movie happens to be very dull," Maggie whispered, trying to pull away from him.

"Maggie, Mike's going to be just fine!"

"There's no story, no character, just a lot of gratuitous sex thrown in to boost ticket sales!" Maggie protested, a little too loudly.

"We know," a little old lady sitting behind Maggie hissed. "Sit down. You're blocking the best parts!"

"How are theater owners supposed to know how we feel about this garbage if we just sit through it?" Maggie asked, jumping up again.

"Or stand through it, in your case," the old lady complained irritably.

Maggie turned to the white-haired woman. "Can it, will you?" she shouted.

"Maggie," Jason pleaded. "Let's just watch the movie, okay?"

Maggie slumped into her seat. She felt the old lady's breath on the back of her neck. "People like you should stay home and watch *The Love Boat*."

"Well, uh, this is the guest room," Mike said to Lisa. As he opened the door, his eyes focused on an old photo of his mother and him when he was five years old. "That about wraps up the tour of the house," he said quickly and chuckled. "Let's go back downstairs and we can watch TV or something." Mike started toward the door, but Lisa pulled him back.

"Let's stay here," she cooed. "It's, like, nice."

"H-h-here?" Mike stuttered. "Uh, what . . . what . . . would we do here? I mean, the . . . the TV downstairs is much more . . ."

Lisa pulled Mike into her arms and silenced him with a passionate kiss on the lips.

When they came up for air, she began kissing his cheek. "Do you have any idea what you're doing to me?" she purred.

"Uh . . . uh . . . well . . . you know, I was just, you know, trying to make my top lip match up roughly with your . . ."

"I mean inside," Lisa said, caressing his ear and pulling him closer.

"Oh, inside? Uh . . . well, you know, I find it's always so hard to say what someone else feels inside" he said. Lisa began to run her fingers through his hair. "And, uh, my Dad, who's, uh, a psychiatrist, he says that . . ." Lisa ran her fingers around his ears and over his face. ". . . Uh, my dad says, uh . . . no two people necessarily have to feel exactly the same inside and . . ."

"I feel all steamy and tingly," Lisa panted.

"I don't specifically remember him mentioning steamy and tingly," Mike said matter-of-factly.

Lisa took Mike's hand and led him to the bed.

"I'll, uh . . . I'll have to ask him about them, . . ." Mike sputtered, and Lisa kissed him again.

Pressing him down on the bed, she began unbuttoning his shirt while she continued kissing him. Mike felt his face begin to freeze.

The steamy kiss ended, but Mike's shocked expression didn't change. Lisa continued to unbutton his shirt slowly, running her fingers gently over his chest.

Mike cleared his throat. "So, Lisa . . . how 'bout that social studies test last Friday?" he asked in a squeaky voice.

Lisa stopped rubbing his chest and sat up. "Mike,"

she said, "I just got, like, a funny idea!"

Mike sat up, too. "F-f-funnier than this?" he asked.

"No, I mean, it just occurred to me . . . like, is this gonna be the first time you've, like, ever done it?"

Mike forced a smile and broke into uncontrollable laughter. He wiped an imaginary tear from his eye and took Lisa's hand. "Lisa, Lisa, Lisa! Heh-heh. Nnnoooooo! I'm sorry that's just too rich! I'm not a virgin, Lisa. Not this cowboy."

Lisa sighed and smiled. "That's a relief," she said. " 'Cause, like, believe it or not, there are guys out there our age who have never done it!"

"Yeah," Mike nodded. "Rejects and nerds."

"Really," Lisa agreed. "So"—she unbuttoned the last button—"where were we?"

"Uh, I'm not sure," Mike sputtered again.

Lisa put her index finger at the top of his chest and slowly ran it down to his belt buckle.

"Ah, now, I remember," Mike said. He turned his head and found himself staring at the photograph of himself and his mother on the night table.

"Did!" Carol shrieked at Ben.

"Did not!" he yelled back.

"Did, too!"

"Did not!"

"I know you did something to Wendy," Carol said, picking up her plant, which stood completely wilted on the living room table.

Ben bit his lip and scratched his head. "I did not!" he said, trying to hide his fear as he lied to Carol.

"Ben, why don't you just admit you killed Wendy, and then I'll kill you and we'll both feel a lot better about the whole thing," Carol said. She flopped onto the couch, holding the lifeless plant.

"No!" Ben shouted as Jason and Maggie walked in the front door. They stood silently while Carol and Ben continued to fight.

"You're a killer and you know it!" Carol yelled.

"I am not!" Ben insisted.

Then Jason signaled, "I'll take this one," and Maggie headed up the stairs.

"Ding!" Jason called, ringing an imaginary boxing bell. He walked over to Carol and Ben. "Just a minute, both of you. Hold it and go to a neutral corner."

"Dad, the plant I was talking to is dead," Carol wailed.

"Well," her father said, "that doesn't bode well for the rest of the family, now, does it?"

"Dad! Ben killed Wendy!"

"I did not!" Ben protested. "Stop saying that!"

"Now, Ben, your sister's not one to make those things up," his father said. "You can look me squarely in the eye and tell me that she's mistaken and then not another word will be said about it. Okay, Ben, did you kill Wendy?"

Ben's eyes moved from his father to the wall. He gulped and looked his father in the eye. "No," he said with difficulty.

Jason turned to Carol, but Ben interrupted.

"Not exactly," he added quickly.

"Aha!" Carol said triumphantly.

Ben's eyes filled up with tears. "Well, I . . . I said . . . a . . . a mean thing to her and a leaf fell off, but I tried to save her. I really tried to save her!"

Jason sat on the arm of the couch and looked squarely at Ben. "How exactly did you try to save her, Ben?" he asked.

"How do you think?" Ben asked, astonished. "With the plant stuff!"

Horrified, Carol reached under the table and grabbed a plastic bottle. She shook the bottle, and her mouth dropped open. "Oh! Oh, my goodness! Ben, did you put the whole bottle on my plant?"

Ben nodded in agreement. "See? I TOLD you I tried to save her," he said.

Jason took the bottle from Carol and read the label. " 'Mix one capful of Mighty Plant with eight gallons of water.' "

"What does that mean?" Ben asked hesitantly.

"Five-to-ten in the greenhouse for you, buddy," his father said tousling Ben's hair. "He didn't do it on purpose, Carol."

Carol shrugged with resignation at Wendy's state.

"Kids?" Maggie called out, coming down the stairs, "Where's your brother?"

"Oh, you mean Mr. Testosterone?" Carol chuckled. "I think he's in the kitchen."

Maggie gave Carol a look and raced out of the living room. She slowed to a walk as she entered the kitchen. "Hey, Mike," she said casually.

Mike was sipping a glass of milk as he absentmindedly leafed through a magazine.

"Mom," he acknowledged, without taking his eyes off the magazine.

Maggie opened a cupboard and took out some cookies. She bit into one. "Where's Lisa?" she asked casually.

"How should I know?" Mike answered, still flipping pages.

"Well, did you two, uh, have a good time together?"

"Sure."

"Oh. What did you do?"

"We hung out."

"Did you, uh, watch any TV?"

"No," Mike said.

"Well," Maggie said, changing the subject, "what's that you're reading?"

"*Windsurfer*."

"Good issue?" she pressed.

"It's not much different from the last eleven issues," he said.

Maggie placed a glass of milk and a plate of cookies on the table and sat down across from Mike. "Are you okay?" she asked.

"Great," he said flatly.

"Good. So, your friend Lisa seems like a very interesting girl," she said, trying to keep the conversation going.

"Yeah, I guess so." Mike snorted.

"What does that mean?" she asked.

"What does what mean?" he said, looking up from the magazine for the first time.

"I said, 'She seems like a very interesting girl,' and you snorted and said. 'Yeah, I guess so.' What does that mean?"

"Well, I guess it means she's an interesting girl."

Maggie chewed on a cookie and wondered how to get the details of the evening out of her son. "So, did you guys . . . play any, uh, board games or anything?"

Mike jumped up from his seat and slammed the magazine on the kitchen table. His eyes filled with tears. "Nothing happened, okay, Mom?" he exploded. "She wanted to sleep with me, and I didn't do it! I'm probably gay. Are you happy now?" With that, Mike turned and started out of the kitchen.

Maggie gasped, then called after him. "Mike?"

He turned. "What is it?" he asked impatiently.

"I'm pretty sure you're not gay," she said.

Mike thought a moment and shrugged. "Yeah, I guess that was a longshot, huh?" He sat back down.

"You know, Michael," his mother said gently, "there's nothing wrong with choosing not to sleep with somebody. I mean, you can even wait for someone you love. People do it all the time."

"Come on, Mom," Mike said bitterly. "It's not like I did some big noble thing here. I just wimped out!"

"Okay, okay, so you 'wimped out,' " she said. "But think about it for a minute. What did you really wimp out of?"

Mike's eyes glazed over as he considered the lost possibilities.

"Let me rephrase that," his mother said. "Do you care about Lisa? I mean, do you care about what she feels or thinks, or if she's happy or sad? Do you really care what happens to her?"

Mike considered the question. "Well, I wouldn't want to see her get hit by a truck," he said.

"And do you think she cares about you?" his mother asked.

"Yeah . . . in the same kind of way," he observed.

"So, you wimped out of sharing something very special with someone who, well, whose face you wouldn't want to see on the grill of an eighteen wheeler," his mother summed up.

"Yeah," Mike agreed. "I guess I see what you mean. But Lisa . . . There was something about her, Mom. She's, she's got . . ."

"Major-league yabos?" his mother completed the sentence. Mike shot her a look of surprise.

"Well, in a nutshell, yeah," he agreed.

Maggie pulled her chair next to Mike's. "Listen," she said with a smile. "Lisa is a great-looking girl. But there are other great-looking girls out there who also happen to be warm, caring people."

"Really?" Mike looked surprised at the thought.

"Yup," his mother said. "And you're going to find one. And when the right girl and the—the right time—come along, I think you'll be feeling anything but wimpy!"

"Yeah," Mike mused. "Maybe you're right."

"Ah, you'll be a little scared at first. But, trust me, you'll find a way to overcome it." Maggie smiled. "Your father did."

"Dad?" Mike asked with surprise and then grinned. "Oh, so I guess you're saying that he waited for the right girl."

"Yes." Maggie shook her head in agreement. "I guess you could say that." She added, "I met her. She was very nice."

Mike smiled skeptically at his mother, and she swatted him with his magazine. "Thanks, Mom," he said sheepishly. "You're all right!"

"Well, thank you, Michael." Maggie smiled again and pulled Mike to her in a bear hug. "You're pretty all right yourself. Why don't you get ready for bed now? It's been a long night."

Mike grimaced and stood up. "You're not kidding!" he said, heading out the kitchen door.

Maggie remained at the kitchen table for a few moments, her head in her hands. "Growing pains!" She sighed. "I guess there's only so much a mother can do!" She turned off the kitchen light and headed for her bedroom.

She met Jason at the top of the stairs.

"Tough night, huh?" he asked as Maggie reached around him in a hug and buried her head in his chest.

"It's not easy being a kid," she said.

"Or a parent for that matter," he said, kissing her on the top of her head. "I'm going to say good night to Mike. I'll just be a minute." He walked down the hall to Mike's room, knocked, and popped his head in the door. Mike was sitting on his exercise bike. "Hey, you okay?" his father asked.

"Yeah, fine, Dad. Really," Mike answered. "This Lisa stuff is history. I'm waiting to hear from a friend about getting tickets to the big Springsteen concert next week. That's really important stuff."

"Okay, Mike, I hope you get the tickets. But you know there are other things that are important besides concerts and girls right now. You've got to start paying attention to your schoolwork. Didn't I hear there's a big history test coming up?"

"Yeah, it's under control, Dad. No problem, thanks. Good night."

"Good night, Mike. Sleep tight."

"Yeah," Mike said, pedaling furiously on the bicycle.

Chapter 3

"When do they outgrow skateboards?" Maggie asked Jason as she watched Mike glide across the kitchen floor on his board, phone in hand.

"When you buy them a sports car." Jason grinned, looking up momentarily from the paper. He sat at the kitchen table with Carol, who was putting the finishing touches on her homework.

". . . Yeah, okay . . . 'Bye," Mike said. He glided across the floor again and hung up the phone.

"So, you're going to see Springsteen, huh?" Jason said, a bit enviously.

"Yep." Mike beamed. "Saturday night. It's going to be awesome. I can just hear it now. 'Ladies and gentlemen . . . Live on Long Island . . . It's THE BOSS!'" Mike rolled up his T-shirt sleeves and turned his back, imitating a Bruce Springsteen stance.

Maggie, Jason, and Carol burst out laughing. Mike jumped onto the kitchen counter and began strumming an imaginary guitar and singing the introduction to "Dancing in the Dark."

"Wait." Carol was still laughing. "Wait. I thought the Springsteen concert was sold out!"

"Sold out?" Mike looked surprised. "Da-nun-na-nun! Carol, to a man with connections, nothing is EVER sold out?" He smiled, pointing toward the telephone. "That just happened to be Seth Jameson, nephew of the man whose brother-in-law runs the hot dog concession at the Coliseum!"

"Wow!" his father said.

"So?" Carol asked skeptically. "Did you get tickets?"

"Did I get tickets?" Mike repeated. "Of course I got tickets!"

"You did?" Carol said enviously. "To Springsteen?"

Mike hesitated. "Uh . . . no. Not to Springsteen. But I did get tickets to the Ice Capades. Darn good seats, too," he added, seeing their expressions change. "And I got two free hot dogs, too!"

"Ooooohhh!" Carol mocked. She picked up her schoolbooks and headed toward the back door. "Talk about connections! Are those all-beef hot dogs?" She rolled her eyes. "C'mon, Ben," she called as she headed for the door, "you're going to be late for school."

"All right. I'm coming," Ben replied from the hall-way. He stomped through the kitchen and grabbed a piece of toast on his way out.

"That's too bad about the concert, honey," Maggie said to Mike once Ben and Carol were gone. "You must be disappointed."

Mike waved his hand. "Nah, I actually have a couple

of other things going.'' He kept his tone upbeat. ''I'll get the tickets. I have to see this concert! It's the event of the year.'' Just then the phone rang. ''All right!'' Mike yelled. ''This is it!'' He leaped off the kitchen counter and grabbed the phone. ''Hello? Yeah. Talk to me. Yeah. Yeah. Yeah. Okay. Yeah. I'll see ya.'' He hung up the phone and slumped into a kitchen chair.

''No dice?'' his father asked.

''No,'' Mike said. ''Jerry was sure we'd be able to get tickets from his friend Cheech, but . . .''

''Cheech?'' his mother interrupted. ''Jason, our son knows people named Cheech?''

''Now, Maggie, you can't judge somebody on the basis of a name. Anyway, Mike, you were saying?''

''Yeah, well, Cheech's parole officer didn't think it was a good idea to be scalping tickets so close to the trial,'' Mike explained. His mother gasped, covering her mouth with her hands.

''Good judgment, there Cheech,'' his father said, trying to keep a straight face.

''Sorry, honey,'' his mother said, patting Mike's hand.

''That's all right,'' Mike said, brightening suddenly. ''I've still got one more shot.'' He picked up the phone, dialed, and waited a moment. ''Yeah, Jimski? It's Mike. Yeah, look. I've got to have those tickets. Yeah. Offer them anything they want. What? My jacket? My leather jacket? The one that smells like actual cattle?'' he asked. A pained expression crossed his face.

Maggie shrugged. ''What can you do?'' she asked.

''He loves that jacket. I even love that jacket,'' Jason answered. ''I never had a jacket that nice.''

Mike nodded as he listened to the voice at the other end of the phone. ''Okay, okay! He can have the jacket!''

His parents exchanged horrified looks. "Oh, come on, Jamie. Look . . . I'd hate to even ask Jerry that. Yeah, all right. Call me right back."

Maggie and Jason looked at Mike quizzically, hoping for an explanation of what he'd hate to ask Jerry.

"He wanted a date with Jerry's sister," Mike explained.

"Trixie!" his mother cried. "She's only eleven!"

"Hey, I said no, okay!" Mike answered defensively.

"Say, Mike." His father got up from his chair. "You don't really want to part with that jacket, do you?"

"No," Mike admitted. "But, Dad, there's no way that Bruce is going to play ten miles from my house and I'm not going to see him. Dad, I've GOT to go to that concert!"

The phone rang again and Mike jumped up nervously. He snatched the receiver off the wall. "Yeah? What? That's impossible," he said dejectedly. "Yeah. Okay. See ya." He hung up the phone and staggered to a chair, looking shell-shocked. "Somebody offered them a house!" he said in disbelief.

"A house?" his mother repeated. "A house for tickets to a Bruce Springsteen concert?"

"Well, just for a weekend, but that's still out of our league . . . unless . . ." He brightened, looking up at his parents. Both shook their heads no before Mike could begin to ask. He sat for a moment, considering their reaction. Then he shrugged, rose, and moved heavily to the green-house door.

"Mike?" his mother called after him.

"Uh-uh," his father said.

"Okay. Fine!" Mike pouted.

"Hey, at least you still have that jacket, right?" his father suggested cheerfully.

Mike made a face. "Who cares? It smells like a dead cow!" He slammed the back door.

"I wish there was something we could do to cheer Mike," Maggie said, as she cleared away the dishes.

"Me, too," Jason said, thoughtfully.

"Oh, well, you know Mike. He bounces back in a hurry!" Maggie laughed. "By this afternoon he'll be into something new. Maybe he'll meet a new girlfriend or get interested in a new sport or a new life-style."

"Well, he bounces back if it involves girls," Jason said. "But Bruce Springsteen? This might be a problem."

"Maybe we could get him that new album the kids are all standing in line for," Maggie suggested. She looked up at the clock. "I'm late for the paper," she said, grabbing her coat. "I'll see if I can find the record at lunch. See you later, honey. Oh! If you have a chance between patients could you pick up some chocolate chips at the supermarket? Carol and I are going to bake cookies." She brushed a kiss on Jason's cheek and flew out the door.

"Sure," he replied to the empty room. He got up from the table, went into his office, and started leafing through a pile of papers. "That name must be here someplace," he mumbled. "Maybe I can help. I'm going to get those tickets if it's the last thing I do!"

"I thought Dad was going to pick them up, Mom," Carol whined, slamming bowls on the kitchen counter. "Now how are we going to bake chocolate chip cookies?"

"He isn't home now, Carol, and they aren't here, so I guess he forgot or was too busy," her mother said. "Anyhow, sugar cookies are good, too. This recipe of my mother's is terrific! You always loved these as a little girl.

Your brothers love them, too! Come on, let's make the best of it.''

"Okay.'' Carol sighed, then she smiled and began taking ingredients from the refrigerator.

"Mom! Mom! Mom!'' Ben shrieked, bolting into the kitchen. "I just saw a mouse in the attic. It was THIS BIG!'' he said, his eyes popping. He held up his hands at least two feet apart.

"Was this a mouse or a small sheep?'' his mother asked.

Ben thought for a moment. "Well, it had beady eyes and a long tail and it went like this.'' He gave his best mouse imitation.

Carol looked up from the mixing bowl. "That's a sheep all right.'' She chuckled.

"Okay,'' her mother said, giving Carol a look. "Now where did we put those mousetraps?'' Maggie began opening doors and drawers around the kitchen looking for the traps.

Carol gasped. "What are you going to do with the mousetraps, Mom?''

"Well, I'll be honest with you, Carol,'' her mother replied as she took some cheese from the refrigerator. "I plan to use them to trap mice.''

"Won't that kill them?'' Carol asked.

Maggie nodded her head. "Hopefully, Carol. A mom's got to do what a mom's got to do!'' Maggie took the bag of traps and waved to Ben. "Son,'' she ordered. "Bring me my Camembert!''

"Awright!'' Ben beamed. "We're going with the big guns!''

"But, Mom!'' Carol cried, starting to get upset. "I mean, they're cute, harmless little creatures.''

"Carol, these are the same guys who carried the plague through Europe in the fourteenth century and killed millions of people!"

Carol shook her head and continued mixing the cookie dough. "That was six hundred years ago, Mom. And besides, you know as well as I do that fleas, not mice, carried the Plague."

"Well, I do know that Carol, but I'm trying to make a point here."

"Which is?"

"I don't want mice in my house!"

Maggie grimaced, turned on her heels, and signaled Ben to follow. They marched out of the kitchen, heading for the attic. As they entered the living room, Maggie noticed Mike lying face down on the couch, a cushion over his head. "Michael?" she called as she walked over to the couch.

"Go ahead, try it," Mike said, with the cushion muffling his voice. "Try to give me some good reason to go on living, Mom."

Maggie thought a moment. "The 'Solid Gold Dancers'?" she suggested.

Mike sat up, threw off the cushion, and gave her a smirk. His mother smiled and shrugged. "Just a thought," she said.

"At least Dad's not here," Mike said. "He'd really try to cheer me up."

"Yeah," his mother agreed, shaking her head in mock disgust. "The slime!"

Mike jumped up from the couch and started pacing anxiously around the living room. "I mean, he always acts like he's going to be real sympathetic, then—before you know it—he turns on you!" Deepening his voice, Mike imitated his father. " 'Mike, Mike, Mike. I find that at times like these it's always best to try to keep a little perspective on life'—aaaaaagggghhhh!" Mike cried, shuddering at his own advice.

"At least he doesn't give you the line about how rough he had it when he was your age," his mother pointed out.

"Whew, that's right!" Mike agreed. "He always says, 'Mike, I'm not going to give you the line about how rough I had it when I was your age. But I think you should be aware that, historically, people have had it tougher than this!' "

Maggie laughed out loud at her son's imitation. Mike slumped in frustration back onto the couch.

As Maggie and Ben started up the stairs toward the attic, Jason hurried in the front door. He slowed suddenly when he saw them. "Hi, honey. Do we have mice again?" he asked, noticing the bag of traps.

"Yep, and if I'm not back in twenty-four hours,"— Maggie leaned over the railing and kissed him—"call a cat!" She bolted up the stairs.

Jason stared after her for a moment. Then he turned and noticed Mike lying on the couch. "Shove over, buddy," his father said, shifting Mike's legs to make room for himself. Jason leaned back. "Mike, Mike, Mike," he said. "Still feeling pretty low, huh, pal?"

"Dad, I'm feeling fine. Let's just drop it, okay?"

Jason put an arm around his son's shoulder and pulled Mike toward him. "Aw, come on, come on! I know what you're going through," he said sympathetically.

"Yeah, sure, Dad."

"No, really. I really do. I mean, I didn't want to bring this up this morning and depress you, but—I have seen Springsteen in concert."

Mike looked at him in surprise. "You have?"

"Uh-huh," his father said. "Ten years ago."

"Really? What was it like?" Mike pressed.

"Amazing." Jason had a faraway look. "I mean, the guy completely blows your doors off!"

"Oh, no," Mike whimpered. "I don't want to hear this!"

"He just made me feel so, so . . ." Jason grasped for words.

"Please, Dad!" Mike moaned, half covering his ears. "Don't!"

". . . so free!" his father added. "I could have just walked right out of that concert and hitchhiked across the country!"

"Stop!" Mike cried. "I can't take this!"

"Oh, sorry," his father said, coming back to reality. Mike glared at him, frustrated by the description of what he would be missing. "Mike," his father said. "If you could have one wish right now, what would it be?"

Mike groaned. "Dad, I'm really not in the mood for this."

"Come on, Mike. Come on, come on, come on. I mean, if you had one thing that would make you the happiest guy in the world, what would it be?"

"The 'Solid Gold Dancers,' " Mike said flatly.

Jason shook his head. "All right, two wishes."

Mike stared into space. "Front row tickets to the Springsteen concert," he said, finally.

Jason's lips burst into a huge grin, and he reached into his pocket. "Well, would seventh row be all right?" he asked sheepishly.

"C'mon, Dad. Don't toy with my emotions," Mike whined, looking at the two tickets his father handed him.

" 'Huntington Dry Cleaners,' " he read out loud. " 'Three shirts, clean, press, no starch.' Thanks, Dad, that was my third wish."

"Ooops!" Jason smiled. "Wrong pocket. How 'bout these?" He reached into another pocket and produced two more tickets. Mike looked away in anguish. "Oh, Miiike," his father sang, holding the two tickets under Mike's nose. Mike turned and looked down at them.

"It can't be!" he shrieked, grabbing the tickets. "Dad, do you know what these are? These are Springsteen tickets!"

"Really?" his father asked with surprise.

"I can't believe it!" Mike said. He ran up and down the living room, kissing the tickets. "I can't believe it! How did you get them?"

"Well, Mike. Your mom and I made a big decision. We could afford either to send you to college or we could get those tickets. What do you think?"

"I think you made the right choice!" Mike said, jumping up and down. "I can't believe it! Two tickets to Springsteen! Wait'll I call Jerry! He's going to freak!"

"Hey, wait a minute," his father called as Mike headed for the phone. "When Jerry finds out we're going, it's liable to kill him."

Mike stopped in his tracks. He turned to his father with a look of surprise.

"We don't want to rub it in," his father said with a grin.

"Right, right," Mike said slowly, suddenly understanding.

"Hey, you don't really mind going to the concert with your old man, do you?" his father asked.

"No, no," Mike said, trying to sound convincing.

"You sure?"

"Yeah, Dad," Mike said, forcing a smile. "This is going to be great!"

"I mean, you don't want to take one of your buddies?"

"No."

"You want to take Jerry?"

"No."

"Your sister Carol?"

"No!"

"Peggy Zelinsky?" his father pressed, teasing.

"No, no! Dad—I want to go with you. Really!"

Jason beamed and grabbed the telephone. "Well, all right then! Let's call Jerry and rub it in!" He laughed. Mike gave him a pained look. "Just kidding," his father said, putting the phone back on the hook.

"I swear it, man, I tried everywhere. There's not one more ticket around," Eddie said. He and Boner were standing by their school lockers.

"Hey, Seaver," Boner called, spotting Mike down the hall. "Did you score the tickets?"

"Hey," Mike said smugly, walking up to his friends. "Did I say I was going to score the tickets? Voilà!" He pulled the concert tickets out of his pocket and flashed them before Eddie and Boner. His friends' mouths dropped open.

"Outrageous, man!" Eddie said. "Where'd you get those?"

"I have my connections." Mike smiled, unlocked his locker, and pulled the door open. Taped on the inside of the locker was a magazine photo of Bruce Springsteen, alongside a revealing profile of Dolly Parton.

"So," Boner said, putting his arm around Mike. "Mikey, buddy, brodsky. Just, ah, how many tickets you got there?"

"Just two," Mike said, pulling his books out of the locker and turning toward his friends.

"What!" Eddie said to Boner. "You think he's gonna take you, bonehead?" Eddie gave Mike a friendly punch in the arm. "He's gonna take me. Right, Mikey?"

"Sorry, guys," Mike said nervously. "No can do."

"Okay, okay, I can respect that," Eddie said, leaning up against the locker door. "Now let me guess—Peggy Zelinsky, right?"

"Oh, man, what an opportunity," Boner agreed. "Have you ever seen a girl after a Springsteen concert? They turn into wild animals!"

"Have you asked her yet?" Eddie asked Mike.

"Nah . . . not exactly," Mike said. "Peggy wants me, man, but she just doesn't do it to me. You know how it is." Mike was stalling, hoping for the bell to ring. It finally did. "Hey guys, there's the bell," he said, slamming his locker shut. "Don't want to be late for English. Gotta go!" He started to move down the hall.

Eddie pulled him back by the arm. "Hey, Seaver, you barely speak English. Who you goin' with, man?"

Mike sighed. "Mfther," he said in a muffled, low voice.

"What?" Boner asked.

"Mfther," Mike repeated, somewhat louder, but still muffled.

"Mfther," Eddie repeated. "Who's mfther?"

"Wait," Boner said. "Is that the new weird kid from Pakistan?"

"No, man," Mike barked. "I'm going with my father!"

Eddie and Boner looked at each other an burst into laughter. "You're gonna see Springsteen with your father?"

Eddie asked incredulously.

"Hey," Mike said, starting to get angry. "My father's not like a 'father,' Okay? He's a cool guy!"

"Yeah, he's cool," Boner said, making a face. "Last time I was over there he was waxing the floor and singing 'Puff the Magic Dragon'!"

"Don't be a jerk, all right, Boner?" Mike growled.

"I'm tellin' ya, Seaver," Eddie said, shaking his head. "It's weird!"

"Hey, look," Mike said. His voice rose. "It's not weird, okay? I mean, just because you're too big a jerk to do anything with your father doesn't mean there's anything weird or uncool about it. And you guys breathe a word of this to anyone and you're dead meat." He turned and stormed down the hall.

"I can hardly believe the big night is here," Jason said. He pulled on a sweatshirt and messed up his hair.

"I think you're even more excited about this than Mike," Maggie said with a smile.

"It's exciting all right," Jason said, looking at his watch. "Mike! Mike!" he called up the stairs. "Let's move it. We want to get a parking spot, and the coliseum will be a zoo!"

"Okay, Dad!" Mike answered. "I'm coming." Moments later, he bounced into the kitchen, strumming an imaginary guitar and singing the Springsteen hit, "Born in the U.S.A." He stopped singing and said, "Ready when you are, Pops." He laughed. "You know, this is going to be fun!"

"Have a great time, you two," Maggie said, kissing them good-bye.

"See you later," they chimed. As they walked into

the garage, they began to sing. They were still singing when the car turned onto the highway, headed to the biggest show in town.

Three hours later, exhausted and exhilarated, Mike and Jason were crushed together in the midst of the excited crowd streaming out of the Coliseum. "Thanks for the tickets, Dad. That was fabulous!" Mike shouted over the noise.

"It was even better than ten years ago," his father shouted back.

"I loved that 'Dancin' in the Dark,' " Mike said. He began to strum his imaginary guitar and croon the tune. Some people around him started to sing along. When Mike finished the song, the crowd applauded.

"It's too bad Mom, Carol, and Ben couldn't have come, too," his father said as they neared the lobby. "But they'll probably get the highlights on the TV news. I wonder if this was filmed for a cable TV special. Did you see all the camera crews?"

"I told you, Dad, this was THE place to be tonight. Thanks again. It was great!" Mike smiled and once again began to sing. This time his father joined him.

" '. . . Can't start a fire—can't start a fire without a spark . . . This gun's for hire . . . dancin' in the dark.' " Strumming their imaginary guitars, Mike and Jason danced through the crowd to the middle of the lobby. One of the many camera crews picked up on them and began following them.

"Excuse me, young man," a female voice said, tapping Mike on the shoulder. Mike spun around, interrupting his duet with Jason.

"I've just been observing the cross-generational appeal of Bruce Springsteen. Did you attend this evening's concert with your father?"

Mike's face froze. "Who wants to know?" he asked hostilely as he spotted the camera focused directly on him.

"All of the tristate area," the woman enthused. "This is *Newsline New York*."

Mike's jaw dropped. His face turned red and he smiled stiffly at the reporter.

"Sir?" she asked Jason. "Is this your son?"

"Hey!" Jason shouted, caught up in the excitement of the music and the crowd. "This big fella here? Not only is this my son, this is my best buddy! Yeow!!" As he shrieked, Jason threw his arm affectionately and dramatically around Mike's shoulder, too caught up in his enthusiasm to notice Mike's expression of horror.

"Tell me, sir, isn't it unusual for a father and son to attend a rock-and-roll concert together?"

"No, no way!" Jason protested, a little too loudly. "Not in our family! Not in any family that loves each other! Right? Bruce! We loved it! Awesome concert! Awesome!" Jason exclaimed, waving toward the camera.

Mike's face was frozen in horror.

Jason pulled Mike close and planted a big, wet kiss on the top of his head.

"Young man," the reporter said, turning to Mike. "Anything you want to say to your friends at school?"

Wide-eyed and furious, Mike ran out of the building. Dumbfounded, Jason turned and watched him run. The camera recorded Jason's confused expression.

Mike stormed toward the car with Jason running after him. "How could you do it, Dad?" Mike said, when Jason caught up with him. He jumped into the front seat and slammed the door fiercely. "How could you?" he repeated.

"Do what?" his father asked in complete ignorance.

He turned the key in the ignition. "I could say the same to you. Why did you run out of there like that? That was embarrassing. We were on TV!"

Mike hid his head in his hands. "Don't remind me," he cried. "I'll be the laughing stock of Huntington High."

"Now wait a minute," his father interrupted. "What's your problem? You wanted to go to the Springsteen concert. I got tickets when no one else could and took you. First you say it was great and you had a swell time, and now you're mad about something." Jason stared at Mike's angry profile.

"You never understand anything," Mike moaned, as Jason maneuvered the car out of the crowded parking lot. "Just get us out of here. I want to go home."

"Mike, Mike, Mike," Jason said. "You're overreacting. The whole thing was a lot of fun."

"Fun? You call that scene with *Newsline New York* fun? Don't talk to me, Dad! Just get me home. I want to die!"

"Carol," Maggie called as she walked into the living room toward the couch where Carol was curled up reading a book. "I was just up in the attic."

"Hey, that's great, Mom," Carol said cheerfully.

Maggie frowned and looked at her daughter. "All the cheese is gone and all the traps have been sprung—but there are no mice in them!"

"Really?" Carol said in amazement.

Maggie plopped onto the couch. "Carol," she said, "I have nothing personal against these mice. It's just that my children's health is more important to me than theirs."

Carol jumped up and threw her book on the coffee table. "Fine!" she said angrily. "Just go ahead and kill them! But where does it stop, Mom? Today it's mice, to-morrow it's the neighbor's barking dog. Then, maybe the mail carrier's late one day. Killing a mail carrier is a federal offense, Mom.'' Carol stormed up the stairs.

"Well, at least she didn't overreact,'' Maggie said out loud. She turned, suddenly, as the front door swung open. Mike stormed in and brushed past her. "Hey, Mike, how was the—concert?'' she asked hesitantly.

Mike grunted and ran up the stairs.

"Is there an irate children's convention upstairs?'' Maggie said to Jason as he walked in the front door.

"What?'' he asked.

"What's with Mike?'' she questioned.

"How should I know?'' Jason said defensively. "He wouldn't say a word to me all the way home.''

"Oh?''

"I guess he thinks I embarrassed him or something,'' Jason said.

"Why?'' Maggie asked. "What did you do?''

"I didn't DO anything!'' Jason shouted. "He's over-reacting. We got interviewed by a television crew and, well, oh, never mind. I'd really rather not talk about it.''

"Oh, well, I'm sure it will blow over,'' Maggie said, hugging Jason. Upstairs, a door slammed, the chandelier shook. "By tomorrow,'' she added. A second door slammed loudly. "Or the day after.''

At breakfast the next morning, Mike grabbed a dough-nut and ran out of the house without saying a word. He had a large shopping bag clutched in his hands.

"I guess he's still angry,'' Jason said as Maggie filled his coffee cup.

"I think embarrassed would be more like it,'' Carol

said. "Dad, did you really have to hug and kiss him on television?"

"It just happened!" Jason said defensively. "We were so caught up in the mood of the concert. It was a real high. How did I know Mike would get so upset?"

"Now, honey, I'm sure Mike knows you didn't mean to humiliate him. But it will take a while for him to get over the fact that you did," Maggie said. "Just give him time. In a few years, he'll be his old self again!"

"Oh, no! Not that!" Carol laughed as she grabbed her books. "I'll try and talk to him at school." She waved and ran out the back door.

Carol walked down the hall toward Mike's locker. Groups of kids were hanging out in front of lockers nearby. She heard several joking about seeing Mike on the evening news.

"So, how's my big brother the TV star?" Carol joked as she approached Mike.

He pulled his head out of the locker and turned around. He was wearing a large black floppy hat and yellow sunglasses. "Knock it off, Carol." he said. "I've been getting that all day! And it's only eight-thirty!"

Just then, Eddie and Boner walked up and opened their lockers. Mike ducked back into his. Eddie pretended to hold up a microphone and turned toward the crowds passing by. "Hello, everbody. This is *Newsline New York*! We're here with Mike and Jason Seaver, two really cool guys!" Eddie and Boner laughed hysterically, punching each other with glee. Then Boner leaned over toward Mike's locker and said loudly, "Stacey wouldn't go out with me to the movies Saturday night, so you know what I did?"

"What?" Eddie asked.

"I asked my dad!" Boner roared.

Mike pulled his head out of his locker. "Hey, Boner! You're really a funny guy!" he said with a smirk.

"Hey, Mikey," Eddie said, putting his arm around Mike's shoulder. "Maybe you and your dad could double with me and my dad some night?"

Mike and Carol turned to leave, but Boner and Eddie stepped in front of them. "Mikey, you can tell us—didja get lucky? Or was that good night kiss all you got?" Boner roared.

"Hey," Carol said with a sneer. "You guys are a lot funnier since your lobotomies."

"Oh, listen to her," Boner said.

"Ooohhh, what a family!" Eddie mocked. "The guy dates his dad, and then gets his little sister to stick up for him. This should make the news, too." He grabbed Boner, imitating Jason's hug of Mike. "What a guy," he mimicked. "We're buddies! Yeow! Yeow! I love this guy! Yeow!" Boner and Eddie pretended to exchange a loud wet kiss and stumbled down the hall, laughing loudly.

Mike sighed in disgust and threw his sunglasses into his locker. He bent down, and reappeared wearing a fake nose and horn-rimmed glasses. "Carol, how am I ever going to get through this!" he groaned as he slunk down the hall.

"I'll never forgive Dad! Never!"

That afternoon, Carol in the kitchen putting the finishing touches on a Save-the-Mice banner. "Come on, Ben," she said. "I need your help to hang this." Ben was stuffing his mouth with potato chips, stopping occasionally for a loud slurp of milk. "The mice need your help!"

"I'm just not political," Ben said, turning his attention to a package of cream-filled cookies.

"Ben, there comes a time when principles alone compel us to take a stand," Carol said seriously. Ben sat silently. "I'll give you a quarter," she offered.

"A dollar," Ben countered.

"Fifty cents," Carol negotiated.

"Deal!" Ben said, nodding his head in acceptance.

"Save the mice! Release the rodents!" Carol and Ben shouted in unison as they marched around the kitchen carrying signs that proclaimed the same messages. "Save the mice! Release the Rodents!"

The parade was still in progress when Maggie and Jason walked in the back door. They put several bags of groceries on the counter and read the signs, shaking their heads in amusement.

Mike gave his father a smirk, pulled off the fake nose, and sat at the kitchen table. Slowly, he removed the horn-rimmed glasses and floppy hat. Then he got up, went to the refrigerator, and took out a pitcher of apple juice.

As Mike poured out a glass of juice, Jason broke the heavy silence in the room. "Okay, sorry," he said. "Dumb joke."

"No, no," Mike said sourly. "You're a laugh riot, Dad." He picked up the glass of juice and headed toward the living room.

"Hey, Mike!" his father called. "Wait! I'm sorry. I know you feel I embarrassed you, and I'm really sorry."

"Yeah, sure, great, Dad."

"Mike, I'm apologizing," his father said. "Don't you think we should get this thing out in the open?"

"Oh, you mean like on national television or something?" Mike asked. "*Newsline New York's* not big enough for you?"

Jason ground his teeth. He remained silent for a few

moments, then, losing his patience, said, "You know, I paid a lot of money for those tickets, and that was so you could go to the concert. I think you're being a little self-absorbed about this . . ."

Mike stared at his father in total disbelief. "I'm being self-absorbed?" he said. "You kissed me on the evening news. Embarrassed me before the tristate area. And I'M being self-absorbed?"

"Well, some people's parents lock them in a closet for seven years!" his father said. "You've got it real tough. YOUR father LIKES you! EEWWW! Cooties! I was just showing my feelings for you. Is there anything so terrible about that?"

"You've got feelings for Mom, too," Mike said, "but you don't go showing them in front of the entire tristate area! Dad, you don't know! I mean, the guys at school . . ."

"Aw, come on, Mike. What do you care what those guys say?"

"That's easy for you to say," Mike shouted. Tears welled up in his eyes. "You don't know what it's like! I mean, they laughed at me because I was going with you! But I defended you! I said, 'My dad's a cool guy!' And then what do you do? You slobber all over me on *Newsline New York*!" Mike turned his head to wipe his eyes.

Jason stood silently, looking down at the floor. He cleared his throat. "All right, okay, Mike, I'm sorry. Maybe we shouldn't have gone to the concert together."

Mike spun around, his eyes red but dry. "Dad! That's not what I'm saying!"

"I mean, maybe you should just have taken a girl,' his father continued.

"Dad! Mike shouted. "You're not listening to me!"

Startled, Jason stopped talking and looked at Mike.

"Look," Mike said. "I'm taking a big risk in telling you this, but I actually like doing stuff with you. I do. I mean, I'm sitting there watching Springsteen with my dad and a lot of other people's parents don't even know what a Springsteen is! All through the concert I was thinking, 'Hey, this is really great!' "

"Yeah?" his father asked quietly, gulping silently.

"Yeah," Mike said, nodding his head.

"I was kind of thinking the same thing," his father said, wiping a tear from his eye.

"Well, maybe there's a way we can both think that . . . without letting the entire free world in on it," Mike suggested.

Jason nodded his head in agreement. "Well, I guess I did lose control a little," he said, pausing for a moment. "Okay, a lot," he added.

"That's all right, Dad." Mike smiled. "I guess Bruce has that effect on people. Maybe next time we should see somebody a little less dynamic."

Jason smiled. "Well, I hear the Osmonds are coming to town," he offered.

Mike looked at his father for a moment, and they both smiled, "Nahhhhh," they said in unison, laughing.

Jason reached toward Mike, then stopped. Instead, he stuck out his hand, and they shook hands briefly. Suddenly, Mike pulled his father toward him and gave him a kiss on the forehead. "I love this guy!" he shouted. "Yeow!"

"You guys," Mike said to his friends as they sat in the living room listening to the latest Springsteen album playing at full blast. "I'm telling you, this does not compare with seeing him live! What a concert! What a musician!

Jason pushed open the door and stuck his head in. "Mike!" he shouted over the blasting music. "Your mother and I are in the kitchen. We're trying to read. . . . You guys think you could turn down, turn down"—he stopped and looked around the living room at Mike's friends—"turn down whoever that is?"

Mike lowered the volume a little, and Jason withdrew his head. Mike looked at his friends with an he's-really-out-of-it expression and waited. As soon as enough time had passed for his father to reach the kitchen, Mike blasted the volume back up and starting bouncing to the rhythm.

"I'm glad everything's back to normal!" Maggie shouted, covering her ears. She looked up from the book she was reading and saw Jason lip-synching to the music and strumming an imaginary guitar.

Chapter 4

"Carol, I need to relax. I challenge you to Trivial Pursuit," Mike said, slamming his history book onto the living room coffee table. He had done all the studying he could handle for one day and now hoped he could persuade his sister to take a break. Mike turned on the radio to break Carol's concentration.

"Did you finish your homework? I finished mine." Carol said.

"What are you my mother? I'm okay. Let's play!"

Carol gave her brother a suspicious look. "Oh, all right. I'm four chapters ahead of the rest of the class, so I suppose I can take a break. Get the game, but I must warn you, you're going to lose."

Mike and Carol sat at the coffee table over the Trivial Pursuit board. "I will not be stopped," Mike said rolling the dice. "Give me your best shot here, Carol, I feel hot.

71

I feel ready!''

Carol drew a card and looked at it. "Okay," she said, smiling slyly. "Heh-heh-heh. Mike, what 1957 Roger Corman film starred Pamela Duncan and Richard Garland?"

"What?" Mike said. "Are they serious?"

"Uh-huh," Carol said smugly, convinced that she had him stumped.

"This sounds worse than a standardized test question or even one of those dumb history quizzes. I know it! *Attack of the Crab Monsters*! That was obvious!" Mike answered. "Come on, gimme a hard question, Carol."

Carol turned the card over to read the answer. "I don't believe it," she said. "You're right."

"Wow—Carol," Mike said suddenly, fiddling with the tuner on the radio. "Remember this song?" The sound of Gladys Knight and the Pips singing "Midnight Train to Georgia" blared out.

"Yeah!" Carol said, jumping to her feet. "Mom and Dad used to play this all the time when we were little!"

"Yeah," Mike said. "Remember what we used to do?" He grabbed a banana from the fruit bowl and held it to his mouth like a microphone. He turned up the radio and tossed another banana to Carol, who caught it and began lip-synching, " 'He's leavin' . . .' "

Mike jumped into the middle of the floor, dancing like a Pip, " '. . . Leavin' . . .' " he joined in.

Together they did their old Gladys Knight and the Pips routine, lip-synching all the words and imitating the movements. They were arm in arm, boogying and singing when Jason and Ben came in the front door. Jason smiled and started dancing along.

Ben watched them, a strange expression of neglect on his face. Then he shook his head, sighed, and headed up the stairs.

Carol sang, " 'I'd rather live in his world . . . than live without him in mine . . .' " and Ben looked back at her from the stairs. " 'Her world . . . is his—his and his alone . . .' "

"I hope this isn't hereditary," Ben scoffed, with a hint of jealousy in his voice.

"Hey, guys!" Maggie called over the sound of the music. She walked into the living room holding a pile of mail. "Report cards!" She held up two envelopes.

Mike flipped off the music, his face blank. But Carol jumped up and down and ran to grab her envelope. As she opened it, Jason and Maggie watched her, smiling at her excitement. Mike hung back near the radio.

"Maggie, we have a child who actually likes getting report cards," Jason said, patting Carol on the back. "Where did we go wrong?"

Maggie smiled as Carol took the card from the envelope. Standing behind them, Mike slowly started to move toward the front door.

"I don't know why I'm so nervous," Carol said, her hands shaking noticeably. "I mean, I already know what I got." She looked at the card. "Yep," she said, starting to read out loud slowly, "A. A." Quickly she added, "A, A, A, and A!"

"Oh, Carol, that's great!" her father cried, hugging her. "Good for you!"

Her mother gave her a kiss, and said "That's wonderful sweetie." Then Maggie turned to hand Mike his report card. She was just in time to see him grab his coat the bolt out the door.

"Mike . . .?" Maggie said as the door closed.

"Where did HE go?" Jason asked.

Maggie shook her head. "I don't know."

"I'll see if I can find him," Carol said and headed out the door.

Jason and Maggie went into the kitchen.

"I'll start dinner," Maggie said.

Jason opened the refrigerator. "I'll do the salad," he said.

They worked in silence.

Carol poked her head in the door. "Sorry," she said, "Couldn't find him." Her head disappeared.

Finally Maggie said, It's been almost half an hour. He's obviously avoiding this. I have to open the envelope."

"I guess so," Jason agreed.

Maggie opened the envelope and scanned the card. Her face fell. "C, C, C, C, D, B," she read out loud.

"Well, he did get one B," Jason said brightly. His jaw dropped when he saw Maggie's expression. "Phys. ed., huh?" he asked.

"You got it," Maggie said sadly, putting down the report card. "What drives me crazy is that—"

"I know," Jason interrupted. "He's not dumb."

"In first and second grade he got very good grades," Maggie recalled.

"Well, that was before Carol came along and started getting excellent grades," Jason said. "The nerve of her."

"I know." Maggie sighed.

"At least he had two great years," Jason quipped.

"Jason . . ." Maggie shook her head.

"Maggie, maybe we're being a little too hard on him," Jason said. "You know, not all kids have to get A's."

"But for the last couple of years it's been getting worse," Maggie said.

"Well, that's what puberty's for." Jason smiled,

shrugging. "You take a difficult situation and you make it impossible."

Just then, Mike walked cheerfully in the back door.

"Mike!" Maggie said sternly. "Where have you been?"

"Oh, I thought I'd go look for Duke." Mike smiled casually.

"Mike," his father said, "Duke ran away six months ago."

"So?" Mike asked in surprise.

"And he wasn't even our dog!"

"Well," Mike said, philosophically, "what does that really mean, Dad? 'Our dog?' I mean, can one living thing ever really OWN another living thing? Maybe I should go look upstairs." He tried to pass Jason and Maggie and leave the kitchen.

"Hey," his mother said, taking him by the arm and leading him to a chair. "I've got a great idea. Why don't we all take a look at what's in this envelope?"

"Oh, okay," Mike said, taking the envelope. He pulled out the card, unfolded it, and read aloud, "If your name is Mike Seaver, you may have already won two million dollars." His parents glared at him.

Mike handed his mother the report card. "Hey look, Mom," he said. "Before you get too upset, ah, you should know that some of these grades might be wrong."

"What scares us is that some of them might be right," his father said glumly as he and Maggie looked over the report card again.

"Hey, I got a C average. That's not bad," Mike said defensively. "It's average."

"Is that what you want to be Mike?" his mother asked, looking up at him. "Average?"

"Well . . . it's a high C, so it's actually a little above average," Mike added.

"Don't they have C-pluses for that?" his father asked.

Mike looked glum. "It's not THAT high."

"You can do better than this, can't you?" his mother asked.

"It's not my fault, Mom. I have a personality conflict with my teacher," Mike said.

Jason shook his head. "Can't buy that, Mike. You have about the same grades in six different subjects with six different teachers!"

"I know," Mike agreed, shaking his head. "The teaching profession just seems to attract people who are difficult to get along with."

"Mike," his mother said. "How many times do we have to go through this? I mean, you're just going to have to work hard."

"I am working hard," Mike said.

"Then why is it that every time I go up to your room when you're supposed to be studying or doing homework, you're either napping or throwing darts?" his mother asked.

Mike thought a minute. "That's how I unwind," he suggested.

"Mike!" his mother said, losing patience.

"Look, Mike, are you saying that you're trying as hard as you can?" his father asked.

"Yeah," Mike said.

"So these C's are honestly the best you can do?"

"No!" Mike said indignantly, "I can get better than C's, Dad."

"Well, Mike, what about this D in geometry?"

"I don't know," Mike said, looking away.

Jason walked over to Mike and put his arm on his

shoulder. "Are the classes too hard for you?" he asked gently.

Mike didn't answer.

"I mean, would you rather be in a math section that's a little . . . less demanding?" his father asked.

"Dad! I can do it!" Mike said, insulted at the suggestion. "Look, I'm passing, aren't I? You don't have to go putting me in with the rejects!" he screamed and stormed out of the kitchen.

"Oh, my." Maggie sighed. "What are we going to do?"

"Be patient," Jason said. "Be patient."

Mike stormed into the living room, where Carol sat, happily looking over her report card. Embarrassed, she put the report card down when Mike came in.

"Hey, Mike, you want to finish our game?" she asked.

Mike looked at her angrily. "Ah, no. I wouldn't want to keep you from admiring your A's," he said sarcastically. "Please. Go ahead. Don't let me stop you."

Carol folded up her report card and put it back in the envelope. "Come on, Mike," she said softly.

Mike snatched the envelope from her hand. "Don't be modest, Carol," he said. "Come on, let's share this special moment." He pulled out the report card. "Oh, I'm so proud of you, Carol," he said with mocking sweetness. "Algebra—A. Social studies—A. Advanced nerdiness—A-plus."

"I am not a nerd," Carol said angrily.

"Hey, Carol, there's nothing wrong with being a nerd," Mike cooed. "I mean, without nerds, who would buy all the back-to-school supplies? Who would date the guys on the math team? And who would raise their hands in class and go, oooh, oooh, oooh?"

"Well, you're just jealous because you never get good grades," Carol said defensively.

"Look, if I studied, I could probably get all. A's," Mike shot back.

"You couldn't even get an A in Lunch-as-a-second-language," Carol said.

"Oh, that's funny, Carol. Have you ever considered being a stand-up comedian? Maybe you could do, like, chemistry comedy and stuff."

"You're such a jerk," Carol said. "If you could get such great grades by studying, then why DON'T you study?"

Mike slumped onto the couch. "Because I have better things to do," he said casually.

"Like what?" Carol asked. "Like getting Lloyd Kreeger to laugh milk out his nose?"

"No, like hanging out with friends, which certain people don't have," he said pointedly.

Carol's face flushed and her eyes filled with tears. "Yeah?" she said. "Well, we'll see just how smart you are on Monday, won't we?"

Mike looked confused. "Why?" he asked. "What's Monday?"

"It's the day the whole school takes the Idaho Standardized Test, stupid," Carol shot back.

"So?" Mike said nervously, trying to cover his fears. "If I study I'll probably get the highest grade in the school."

"You can't study for this test, bonebrain," Carol said, enjoying her one-upmanship. "It's an aptitude test."

"I know," Mike said, adding, "what's an aptitude test?"

"Basically it's an IQ test to see how smart you are," Carol explained. Mike's face darkened. "Or, in your case,"

Carol added, "how smart you aren't." She stood up and walked toward the stairs.

Mike slumped further into the couch cushions.

On Monday morning Mike sat at his desk, drumming his fingers. He was trying not to appear nervous as Mr. Lipstone, a crusty old teacher, prepared to hand out the standardized-test forms.

"All right now, listen up," Mr. Lipstone shouted over the din of chatter in the classroom. "This is the Idaho Standardized Test . . ."

"Oh, I hate these tests!" Roy Rosenstock hissed under his breath to Mike, who was sitting next to him. Shaking with nervousness, Roy kept adjusting his glasses and clearing his throat as the teacher walked up and down the rows of desks. "I hate number two pencils. I hate this whole experience," Roy cried softly, his eyes filling with tears.

Mike looked over at Roy and, fueled by anxiety, started drumming his fingers faster and harder on his desk. "Hey, look, calm down," he said, trying to appear cool. "This isn't such a big deal."

"Not a big—not a big deal?" Roy croaked. "Tell that to the hives that are breaking out on my thighs!"

Mike's eyes widened. "You get hives on your thighs?" he asked.

Roy started to roll up the leg of his pants. "You want to see them?" he asked.

"No, no," Mike said quickly. "I believe you!"

Mr. Lipstone reached Mike's desk. He dropped a computer answer-sheet in front of Mike and another in front of Roy.

"Oh, my gosh!" Roy gasped.

"Relax," Mike said, looking over the answer sheet.

"This test doesn't even count on our grades. I mean—what difference does it make what we get?"

"Are you kidding?" Roy said. "This is an IQ test. This is ten times more important than our grades."

Mike's face froze in terror. "Whhaaa . . . what are you talking about?" he said.

"This test decides once and for all how smart we are. I mean, after today our parents will know how stupid we are. Our brothers and sisters will know how stupid we are. I can only assume the entire state of Idaho will know how stupid we are!" Roy blurted.

Mike sat petrified. "Our . . . PARENTS get these results?" he asked incredulously.

"I'll never hear the end of it." Roy moaned. " 'Poor Roy,' " he said, mimicking his parents. " 'He's just not as bright as his brother David. Our David is prelaw at Princeton this year. Oh, hi, Roy, could you take out the garbage, please? We're hoping you can do it professionally some day.' "

"Hey, look," Mike said, "what do you care about your brother? So he's a nerd. Every family's got a nerd."

"Oh . . . yeah, that's right. You've got Carol. She's a genius," Roy said, nodding. "You're going to look like a tree stump next to her."

"No, I'm not," Mike said. "Because for one thing, I'm just as smart as she is. And for another thing, I happen not to believe in these tests." He held up the answer sheet. "I mean, you know what I do?" he asked Roy as he began randomly filling in the computer spaces on the sheet.

Roy started to hyperventilate, his eyes widening.

"I don't even read the questions." Mike said. "I just fill in these computer dots in a pretty pattern. Like this." He filled in a few more spaces and held the answer sheet at arm's length, studying the pattern.

"All right," Mr. Lipstone called from the front of the room. "You may begin!"

"Are you crazy?" Roy cried to Mike. "What are you doing?"

"Oh, I call this a self-portrait." Mike smiled. "They'll love it in Idaho."

"All right, Mr. Ellis," Jason said as he finished a session with a patient in his office. "Is there, ah, anything else you'd like to talk about before we stop for today?"

"Nope," Mr. Ellis replied cheerfully, sitting on the edge of the analysis couch. "Everything's just great!"

"Good. Okay, then," Jason said. "Well, ah, I think we're making some real progress with your problem."

"What problem is that?" Mr. Ellis asked.

Jason took a deep breath. "Well, Mr. Ellis, we both know, don't we, that you're an habitual liar."

"No, I'm not."

"Now, Mr. Ellis . . ."

"Okay, okay," Mr. Ellis said. "Don't pressure me like this. My whole life is going down the drain!"

"Ah, now, but just a minute ago you said everything is just great," Jason reminded him.

"No, I didn't," Mr. Ellis said.

"Well, then," Jason said, standing up and escorting Mr. Ellis to the door, "we certainly do have a lot to talk about next time, don't we?"

"What next time?" Mr. Ellis asked. "I'm never coming back here again!"

"Fine," Jason said. He opened the door for Mr. Ellis to leave, "Whatever you say . . ."

"Fine," Mr. Ellis said, waving good-bye. "See you

next Wednesday?''

"Good. Yeah." Jason said, shaking his head and closing the door. He turned and saw Ben sitting on the living room couch, reading a comic book. "All right, Ben," he said. "Let's do it!"

"Aw, Dad," Ben said awkwardly.

"Come on, Ben," his father chided. "I don't ask you to do much around here, but when I do, I expect it to get done."

"But, Dad . . ." Ben protested.

"Without an argument," his father insisted.

"Can't I do it later?" Ben asked.

"Ben," his father said, "you're testing me now."

"Awright," Ben said. He got off the couch slowly and moved toward the middle of the living room.

"That's more like it!" Jason smiled and gleefully pushed the "play" button on the tape recorder. The sounds of Gladys Knight and the Pips boomed around the room. Jason jumped to the middle of the floor, next to Ben, and started teaching him the Pips' routines while the music blasted in the background. "Ah, Ben, you're a born Pip!" Jason beamed as he flung his arms back and forth to the beat.

"What's a Pip?" Ben asked.

"It's a state of mind." Jason smiled, illustrating an arm motion.

The ring of the telephone interrupted the nostalgic music. Quickly, Ben snatched up the phone. "Hello? Okay, wait a second," he said, handing the receiver to his father. "It's for you."

Jason put the receiver to his ear. And Ben headed for the stairs.

"Yoo, Ben," his father called after him, stopping Ben

in his tracks. "Don't go away now. We're not done."

Ben walked back toward the tape recorder.

"Hello?" Jason said into the phone. "Well, no, my wife is at work. . . . Well, yes, oh, yes, of course, if it's that important. All right. I'll see you then." He frowned as he hung up the phone. "Hey, Ben," he said, pointing to the tape recorder. "Will you turn that off please!" He picked up the phone again and dialed. "Yeah, Maggie?" he said into the receiver. "Can you meet me down at the high school in about half an hour? . . . Well, Dr. Marlens, the school psychologist, just called. It's about Mike."

Jason and Maggie met in front of Dr. Marlens's office. "What's this all about?" Maggie asked, as she raced breathlessly up to Jason. "I had a deadline to make when you called. What happened?"

"I don't know," Jason said, taking her by the arm. "But Dr. Marlens sounded very concerned. He said this couldn't wait."

When Maggie and Jason entered the school psychologist's office, Dr. Marlens was nervously twirling a roll of breath mints and a roll of antacids. "Ah, Dr. and Mrs. Seaver, yes, I've been waiting for you," he said. "Please have a seat. We have some concern over"—he paused momentarily. "Breath mint?" he asked, offering one of the packages. "No? Okay—concern over the results of Mike's IQ test."

"Why?" Maggie asked. "What did he score?"

"Now, Maggie," Jason said, patting her arm. "You know these are highly subjective. Many diagnosticians . . . they don't even consider that to mean—" Jason stopped as he took in Dr. Marlens's depressed expression.

"What DID he score?" Jason asked.

Dr. Marlens sighed deeply. "He scored—well, let me just put this in context for you, Mrs. Seaver. Now, a score of one hundred is about average. One-twenty is very bright. One-forty is considered a genius. One-sixty is—"

"What did Mike score?" Maggie interrupted.

"Twenty-seven," Dr. Marlens said.

Maggie jumped to her feet. "What?" she shouted. "This is ridiculous! I mean, this is obviously a mistake!"

"I'm sorry, Mrs. Seaver. Mike definitely scored twenty-seven." He offered Maggie a Digel. "Antacid?"

"No," Maggie said angrily.

"Twenty-seven?" Jason repeated.

"I'm glad that you're a psychiatrist, Dr. Seaver," Dr. Marlens said, turning to Jason. "You'll understand what I'm saying here . . . "

"You're saying my son is an idiot!" Jason shouted.

"No," Dr. Marlens said, "Technically, he's an imbecile."

Maggie jumped to her feet. "What?"

"Well," Dr. Marlens explained matter-of-factly, "zero to twenty-five is an idiot."

"Well, that's certainly a load off MY mind," Maggie said sarcastically.

"Let's see," Dr. Marlens went on, lost in his own train of thought. "I believe that sixty to seventy is a moron—no, wait—what's fifty to sixty?"

"I don't know," Jason said, losing patience, "A Bozo?"

"No. Well, never mind." Dr. Marlens cleared his throat. "This has nothing to do with Mike."

"No, no, because according to this," Jason said, "Mike could never even aspire to becoming a bozo."

"Oh, now, Dr. and Mrs. Seaver," Dr. Marlens said,

"the worst thing we can do is overreact to this. Has Mike taken a sharp blow to the head?" he asked.

"No!" Maggie said emphatically.

"Suffered any . . . prolonged oxygen deprivation?" Dr. Marlens probed.

"No! Dr. Marlens, our son is not brain-damaged," Jason said.

"O—kay," Dr. Marlens said. "Just checking. Now look," he continued, sighing deeply. "Mike's file indicates that he's always had, how shall we say, a problem with authority." Jason and Maggie looked at one another. "For example, it says here"—Dr. Marlens picked up a folder— "that last year he placed a litter of gerbils"—Dr.Marlens hesitated, trying not to laugh—"into Mrs. O'Brien's tissue box . . . and when she went to blow her nose . . . Ha-ha-ha . . ." Dr. Marlens chuckled helplessly. "That old bag must have just . . ."

Maggie and Jason glared at the psychologist, who coughed uncontrollably, trying to dispel his hysterics. He resumed his serious demeanor.

"Excuse me," he apologized. "There's so little joy in my job. And"—he pointed to Mike's file—"he's got a lot of good stuff in here."

"Thank you," Jason said stiffly. "Dr. Marlens, what are you getting at here?"

Dr. Marlens held up a computer answer-sheet. "You see this?" he asked. "This is a normal test-answer-sheet. It's a mess. The little dots are scattered randomly around the page." He held up a second answer-sheet. "You see this? This is your son's test-answer-sheet. The dots form little pictures of houses, airplanes—and look here—there's even a young woman's profile." He looked more closely at the sheet. "Nice figure," he observed.

Maggie and Jason looked at Mike's answer-sheet and then at each other.

"So you're saying—you're saying that Mike did this—intentionally?" Maggie asked.

"Either that, Mrs. Seaver, or he's a highly artistic imbecile," Dr. Marlens concluded as he placed the answer-sheet back in Mike's folder.

Mike was alone in the living room, plunking on his guitar, when Carol walked in. "What's that you're playing?" she asked. "It's pretty."

Mike stopped playing. "Nothing," he said sullenly.

Carol shrugged. "I heard you got called down to the school psychologist today," she said, biting into an apple and slumping into her favorite overstuffed chair.

"Oh, yeah," Mike said casually. "Mom and Dad are there right now."

"They are? What did you do?"

"Oh, I got a twenty-seven on my IQ test," Mike said.

Carol gasped, and swallowed a bite of apple. "Oh, well, you know," she said reassuringly, "Mom and Dad don't really care about that sort of thing—you know—don't feel bad." She stopped talking and chomped on her apple for a moment. Then she said in disbelief, "You got a twenty-seven?"

"Yeah." Mike shrugged. "I did it on purpose, bonehead. I mean I didn't even read the questions."

"What?!" Carol shrieked.

"Hey," Mike said, gesturing with his hands, "I know I'm brilliant, so I figured, why waste my valuable time on playing fill-in-the-dots?"

"Come on," Carol said skeptically. "You didn't really do that?"

"Carol, Carol, Carol," Mike said, sounding like his father. "How should I put this. . . . You see, before you were born, Mom and Dad came to me and they said, 'Mike, we hope that our next child isn't some goody-goody nerd-face. We hope he'll be a real, independent freethinker like you.' "

"Yeah." Carol smirked. "Little did they know you had peaked intellectually."

The back door slammed shut. Carol and Mike both turned at the sound.

"Mike!!!" Maggie called from the kitchen.

"They're gonna kill you!" Carol warned.

"Carol, maybe Mom and Dad have realized how stupid these tests are," Mike said. "Maybe they're gonna admire me for what I did."

Jason and Maggie entered the living room together. Their faces were dark with anger and concern. "Mike?" his father said menacingly. "Could we speak to you in the kitchen, please?"

Without waiting to see that Mike followed, Jason and Maggie went back to the kitchen.

"Maybe they're going to have you killed profession-ally," Carol said as she turned and ran upstairs.

After Carol left, Mike hesitated in the living room, trying to decide what to do. He considered bolting out the door, but knew he'd have to face them sometime. "Here goes," he said and headed for the kitchen.

When he pushed open the kitchen door, he saw Jason and Maggie slumped wearily at the table.

"Mike," his father said, "can you explain to us what this is?" He held up the computer answer-sheet.

"Oh, okay," Mike said cheerily. "Uh, this here is a Boeing seven-forty-seven. And this is a largemouth bass.

And this''—he paused and smiled broadly—''this is a full-body profile of Rhonda Tishkin. Pretty good likeness, don't you think?''

Maggie scowled, her eyes filling with tears. ''Mike, why did you do this?'' she demanded.

''She's got a great body, Mom.'' Mike smiled.

''Mike, this isn't a joke,'' his father said. ''C'mon, why did you do it?''

Mike slumped into a chair. ''I don't know,'' he admitted. ''I just felt like it.''

''You just felt like it . . . '' his mother repeated.

''Well, gee, I didn't realize how important these tests were to you guys. Maybe you should have told me you were only interested in having kids with high IQ scores,'' Mike said. He stormed out of the kitchen.

Maggie and Jason jumped up and followed him into the living room.

''Mike . . .'' his father started.

''That's okay, that's okay,'' Mike yelled. ''I mean, you guys have one smart kid. Your Miss Straight-A's can go and become an astronaut, and Mikey can always go and mix the Tang—no problem!'' He ran out the front door, slamming it hard behind him.

''Mike!'' his mother called after him.

''Why don't we just let him cool down,'' Jason said as he put his arm around Maggie, who was trembling. ''I think he's been trying to tell us something. Now we know what it is.''

Mike stormed across the front lawn and paced around the block, kicking at the grass. Then he slowed down and walked back to the porch. He sat in the porch swing and began rocking sullenly. After a few minutes, he looked up and saw Carol standing at the front door watching him.

"What do you want?" he asked angrily.

"Nothing, really," she said hesitantly. "I mean . . ."

"Well, then why don't you just get out of here," Mike hissed.

Carol started to leave but turned back toward Mike. "Look, Mike . . . you're not really stupid," she said floundering for the right words.

Mike looked at her incredulously. "Well, thanks, Carol. I'm deeply touched by your superiority."

"I hope I don't make you feel stupid, Mike," Carol said, trying again.

"You DON'T make me feel stupid. Just get out of here, okay?" Mike yelled. "Nobody makes me feel stupid, because I'm not stupid!"

"I just said that," Carol pointed out.

"Well maybe I was just too stupid to understand," Mike said sarcastically.

"Mike, come on," Carol pleaded. "I mean, you're always calling me a nerd and stuff . . . and, I don't know, I guess I was just trying to get you back—I guess because you're older and popular and cooler and everything. . . . And . . . and . . . I just felt that I was the only one who was getting hurt," she continued.

Mike looked at her but said nothing.

"I mean, I AM sort of a nerd, but you're not really stupid," Carol said.

"So," Mike said bitterly. "I guess it's just a coincidence that you get all the A's and I get all the C's?"

"Look, I don't know why you don't get good grades," Carol said. "I mean, well, maybe it has something to do with the fact that you sleep or play darts while you're doing your homework."

"What is it with the darts?" Mike asked. "Am I the

only guy around here who knows how to unwind?''

"Okay," Carol said. "Listen. What year did Max Weinberg start playing drums for Bruce Springsteen?''

Mike looked at Carol in confusion. "Hey, did we just start a new conversation?" he asked.

"Come on, come on, what year?" she pressed.

"It was 1973," Mike said. "So what does that mean?''

"Well . . . aside from meaning a huge boost in income for Max Weinberg, it means you're pretty smart," Carol said.

"What? 'Cause I know one useless fact?''

"You know MILLIONS of useless facts! I mean, like the *Attack of the Crab People* thing!" Carol said. "I mean, I couldn't believe you knew that!''

"*Crab Monsters,* Carol," Mike corrected. "*Attack of the Crab Monsters.*''

"See? I mean, you don't remember things for tests, you just remember things you want to remember . . . for some . . . strange . . . reason.''

Mike shrugged. "So I have a good memory. Big deal.''

Carol shook her head. "It's more than just that. OKay, remember last year when you borrowed twenty bucks from me on Valentine's Day?''

"Yeah?" Mike recalled. "So?''

"And I made you sign an IOU?" Carol said.

Mike smiled at the memory. "Which I gladly did.''

"Yeah," Carol said, "promising to pay me back on February twenty-ninth.''

"Hey," Mike said, laughing, "come 1988, that twenty bucks is yours!''

Carol smiled ruefully. "You see, that . . . that wasn't just intelligent, that was actually very . . . creative," she pointed out.

"You were just a sucker," Mike said, dismissing the incident.

"That's my point. I mean, I do dumb things all the time. And you do smart things—when you feel like it."

"Well . . ."

"Hey," Carol interrupted, "why do you think Mom's always telling you to shut up your smart mouth? I mean, it takes brains and hard work to be as obnoxious as you are."

"Yeah, I guess it does." Mike nodded in agreement. "But when you love what you do, it really doesn't seem like work."

Mike and Carol smiled at each other.

"I mean, heck, for all we know," Carol said, "you and I might even have the same IQ."

"Yeah," Mike agreed. "Who knows? Mine might be even higher!"

"Let's not get hysterical, now." Carol grimaced.

They looked at each other again and chuckled.

"Carol?" Mike said.

"Yeah?"

"Thanks."

Carol shrugged. At the same time, Mike stuck out his hand. She smiled and moved to shake hands. Instead, Mike ran his hand up to her face and bopped her on the chin. "You jerk." She laughed.

"Nerd." Mike smiled, adding hastily, "I meant that in a nice way."

They both laughed then hugged each other.

Maggie and Jason, peering out the window behind them, smiled.

Later that afternoon the Seaver family was gathered around the kitchen table, when the telephone rang. Jason picked up the phone. "Uh-huh. Oh good. Thank you. Yes. Thank you very much. All right. Bye-bye." He hung up the phone and turned to Mike. "Hey, Mike. Dr. Marlens says you can take that Idaho test over again Saturday morning, ten o'clock."

Mike grimaced. "Oh, that's great, Dad. But, uh, I've been thinking about it and, uh, well, I'm kind of happy with the twenty-seven."

Jason glared at Mike, who muffled a smile. "Mike . . ." Jason said sternly.

"Yes, Dad, okay. Maybe this time I'll top thirty!"

Saturday dawned crisp and clear. Mike awoke early. He dressed in jeans and a Springsteen sweatshirt, and headed to the kitchen for breakfast.

"Ready for the test?" Jason asked casually. "Just play it straight and do your best. I know you'll do fine."

"Yeah, Dad. I really am sorry about that twenty-seven business. I guess I just panicked and figured I'd laugh my way out of it."

"That wasn't much of a laugh, Mike," Jason said, pouring some orange juice. "There's a time for fooling around—I'm all for that—but there's also a time to concentrate and set priorities. Doing well in school is one of them. Just give it your best shot."

"I will, Dad, really. After Carol showed me how much I know about weirdo facts, I figure this shouldn't be as hard as I thought." He grabbed a doughnut on his way to the back door. "See you guys later!" he called as he ran through the greenhouse.

Chapter 5

"I'm exhausted," Maggie said as she sprawled on the living room couch, glancing through the newspaper. "I hope Mike learned his lesson."

"Me, too," Jason agreed. "It's been a long day." He leaned his head back on his chair and closed his eyes. "I love the silence." He smiled. "I love the crinkly sound of the pipes and the creaky floors."

"Me, too." Maggie smiled. "This feels wonderful."

Suddenly the silence was broken. The sound of a dull bass pounded overhead. Maggie and Jason looked up at the semimusical sound and sighed. Tiny bits of plaster were falling like snowflakes from the ceiling.

"So much for silence." Jason grinned.

"So much for creaking floors," Maggie said. "I just hope the ceiling holds up."

Jason nodded his head in agreement. Then he said, suddenly, "Two years, six months, and two days."

"What?" Maggie, looked at him in surprise.

"That's how long we have until Mike goes to college," he explained.

Maggie smiled and shook her head.

"Hi, guys," Ben mumbled, coming in from the kitchen with a doughnut in his mouth. He carried a platter piled high with junk food. "Time for some serious TV watching." He plopped down next to Maggie, spilling pretzels on the couch, and pushed the rest of the doughnut into his mouth. Then he picked up the remote control device and turned on the TV set.

Maggie looked toward Jason.

"Nine years and six months," she computed, pointing to Ben. Jason shook his head. "Ben, turn that thing down," he said. "Your brother is trying to study. He has a big history test on Tuesday." Ben gulped down a mouthful of doughnut and looked up at the ceiling. Bits of white plaster were still drifting down. He turned to his father. "You call that studying?" he asked and turned his attention back to the TV screen.

"Mike!" Jason called upstairs. "Turn down that noise! You have to study for the test!"

"Okay, Dad!" Mike yelled. He lowered the sound on his tape player a tiny bit and leaned back in his desk chair. The small desk was piled high with schoolbooks, magazines, and assorted garbage. Soda cans balanced precariously on top of boxes of cookies and pretzels. Piles of dirty clothing surrounded the desk.

Mike tapped out a tune on the desk with his hands, like a drummer, as the loud music bounced off the walls. At the same time, he covered a page of his history book and began to quiz himself. "The commander of the Confederate Army was," he said out loud, tapping on his desk as he considered the answer, "Bruce Lee."

He uncovered the answer and read it out loud, "Oh, Robert E. Lee. Close." He looked down at the book and chose another question. "The Civil War started in 1861 and lasted . . ." He thought a moment and added, "far too long." Checking his text, he frowned. "Oh, not even close this time! Darn!"

Mike swung around on his chair and caught a glimpse of himself in the bureau mirror. He smiled broadly. *You are sooooo cool*! he said to himself.

"Are you talking to me?" he asked out loud.

I'm the only one here! He laughed as he pushed his fingers through his hair and pulled up the collar of his shirt.

A knock at the door startled him.

"I'm studying, so leave me alone, scuzzball!" he called through the door.

His father walked into the room. "Scuzzball?" he said.

"Oh, Dad. Sorry. I thought you were Ben. I'd never call you scuzzball to your face!"

Jason frowned and looked around the room. "Mike," he said, "it looks like a tornado went through this place. I thought you'd told me you were going to clean your room."

Mike looked surprised. "I did clean it!" he protested.

"Nice," his father said, closing his eyes for a moment. "Isn't this music still a little loud?"

"Absolutely," Mike agreed.

Jason walked across the room, climbing over piles of dirty towels, and shut off the tape player.

"Dad!" Mike said in astonishment. "What are you doing? I'm trying to study."

Jason climbed back over the piles of towels and stood

by the door. "Mike, I sure don't want to change the study method that has kept you on the brink of failure all year," he said. "But for the sake of the plaster on the ceiling of the living room, I'd like you to study for this history test without music or any other loud distraction."

Mike looked doubtful. "Boy, all that silence could really throw a guy off," he said.

"Let's risk it." his father proposed. "Just you and the book for a solid hour. No music or whatever that was."

"What is this?" Mike asked defensively. "Are you pressuring me for a good grade?"

"No," his father said. "I'm a realist. I'm pressuring you for a passing grade. Look, so far this year you've made it through American history with a sixty-seven . . ."

"No," Mike interrupted proudly, "a sixty-eight!"

Jason sighed. "With this exam, you can really do something about raising that. Why not aim for the stars? Seventy? Seventy-five, even!"

"Dad, I get the feeling that you don't think I know this stuff," Mike said, tapping on his desk again.

Jason glanced at Mike's history book. "Abraham Lincoln was assassinated . . . ?" he asked.

Mike gulped. "True," he answered.

"The date, Mike, the date!" his father said.

"I could answer that," Mike said. "But that would only prove something to you! What's important is that I prove something to me!"

"Mike," his father said softly, "a wise man once said that those who don't know their history are doomed to repeat it."

Mike's eyes widened. "You mean like in summer school?" Jason reached for the doorknob and turned it. "Exactly," he said. He closed the door and left Mike alone with his history book.

Mike looked down at the closed book. "Abraham Lincoln was assassinated," he said out loud, "while he was still alive!" He spun around and again looked at himself in the mirror. He flashed a thumbs-up sign and smiled. "Did I mention," he said to his reflection, "that you are SO cool?"

"If we're out of apples, what do you want?" Maggie called to Jason in their bedroom as she stepped into the darkened hall two nights later.

"A piece of chocolate cake," he called back. "With extra frosting."

"We'll probably have one rotten apple, and I'll get stuck with it," Maggie mumbled to herself as she moved toward the stairs. Suddenly she noticed a slit of light streaming from under Mike's door. She leaned back into the bedroom and whispered loudly, "Jason! Come quick!"

Jason jumped from the bed and ran over to her. "What? What's the matter?" he asked anxiously.

"Look!" Maggie pointed toward Mike's door. "Wow! Mike must be studying. What do you know? I actually got through to him the other night!" He beamed.

"Yes," Maggie agreed. "That must be it. You probably got him so fired up he's dizzy with the thirst for knowledge."

Jason tiptoed to Mike's door. "Just listen," he whispered to Maggie. "Mike?"

"Yeah?" Mike answered from inside the room.

"What are you doing?" his father asked.

"Why?" Mike said suspiciously.

"I'm curious," Jason said to the closed door. "Are you studying?"

"Oh, yeah," Mike said. "There's no way I'm going to flunk this test."

Jason turned to Maggie, smiling an I-told-you-so grin. Then he called to Mike, "Good. That's good, Mike."

"Jason," Maggie whispered loudly. "Somebody's in that room imitating Mike's voice."

"Very funny, Mom," Mike whispered back through the closed door.

"Good night, Mike," his parents called as they walked away from the door.

"I'll take that chocolate cake now, even if we have apples," Jason said to Maggie. "This is a cause to celebrate." Maggie smiled and tiptoed down the stairs to the kitchen. Jason walked happily back to their bedroom.

"Whew, that was a close one," Mike said. He had listened through the door until he'd heard the sound of his parent's footsteps fade away. "Okay, Carol. Let's get on with this." Mike stretched out on his bed, his hands clasped behind his head.

Carol sat at Mike's desk, his history book cradled in her lap, yawning repeatedly. "Mike?" she said, between yawns. "The answer?"

"I'm very close," he said.

"Come on," Carol said. "I'm very tired."

"Hey, Carol, this is no picnic for me, either," Mike protested.

"A general, Mike. Just name ANY American general," Carol said.

Mike hesitated. "General—Motors?"

Carol stood up and slammed the book shut on Mike's desk. "That's it! I'm going to bed," she announced.

"Bed?" Mike said, jumping up from his. "How can

you think of bed at a time like this?''

"Mike, it's hopeless. You can't learn all this in only three days,'' Carol said. "You should have been studying for this when you went camping or dirt-biking or whatever. You waste your time and then panic at the last minute. Watching you wallow in your ignorance is too demoralizing,'' she concluded. "Good night!''

Mike jumped to block Carol from leaving. "If you're so good at it, how do YOU study?'' he asked.

"It's very simple,'' Carol explained, yawning again. "I read the material when it's assigned. I underline key phrases, I take careful notes, and I quiz myself.'' She released herself from Mike's grip and walked out of the room.

Mike's face lit up in inspiration. "Of course!'' he said out loud. "Underlining!''

"Kids! Let's move it!'' Jason called the next morning as he put the finishing touches on a breakfast plate and placed it on the table before Maggie. "Everybody's late this morning,'' he said. Maggie yawned in response.

A few yawns later, Maggie said, "Every time I turn on Ted Koppel, I know I'm going to lose sleep.'' She looked suspiciously at the plate before her.

"Hi!'' Carol called as she came into the kitchen. She put her schoolbooks on the counter.

"Where have you been?'' her father asked. "Breakfast is ready!''

"Sorry,'' Carol said. "I was up late—studying.''

"Do you have a test, too?'' her mother asked. Maggie poked her fork around her plate.

"Nope,'' Carol said.

"See?'' Jason said to Maggie. "Mike could learn from her.''

"No, he couldn't," Carol said. She glanced at the breakfast Jason had made, picked up her books, and headed off to school. " 'Bye. See you tonight," she called.

Maggie pushed back her chair and picked up her briefcase. "Well, I hate to eat and run," she quipped.

"You didn't finish your breakfast!" Jason said with disappointment.

"Well . . . " Maggie hesitated, busying herself with her papers and moving from the table. "What I ate was very filling, but . . ."

"Now don't give me that!" Jason interrupted. "You don't have to make up some story. If you didn't like the breakfast, just say so."

"Jason . . ." Maggie began.

"I can take it," Jason said, pushing back his shoulders and standing taller.

"Well, I—"

"Go ahead, say it," Jason interrupted again.

Maggie sighed. "It was dreck."

"Okay, then. That's better," Jason said.

Maggie kissed him on the cheek and picked up her briefcase. "Just kidding," she apologized.

"All of it, or just the eggs?" the deflated chef asked.

"Those were eggs?" Maggie said in astonishment and ran out the back door.

Jason sighed. "They looked good to me," he said out loud.

Just then, Mike bounced into the kitchen carrying his books and a large brown paper bag. "Okay." He beamed at his father. "Say good morning to God's gift to history." He sat down and began to eat heartily, placing the paper bag on the table in front of him.

"Hey." Jason smiled. "You look like a guy who's

ready for a history exam!''

"Ready? I'm not just ready, Dad. I've got it all!"
Mike said with assurance. "Names, dates, everything. I
think this day will go down in history as the day Mike
Seaver turned the corner—Wednesday, Febru—"

"It's Tuesday," Jason interrupted.

"Close enough." Mike laughed.

Ben came into the kitchen. "Hey, Dad," he said.

"Hey, Ben."

Ben sat down at the table and took one look at the
eggs. "This is breakfast?" he asked, with a grim look.

"Yep." Jason smiled.

"What's in my lunch?" Ben asked.

"A surprise," his father said mysteriously. "Enjoy!"
He picked up a stack of papers and headed toward the
swinging door. "I have some phone calls to make, guys,"
he said. "Eat your breakfasts and get out in time for your
school buses. I'll see you tonight." He walked out of the
kitchen to his office.

Ben looked down at the plate in front of him. "Uh-
oh," he said, starting to taste the food. "I hate surprises."
He picked up the brown bag on the table, opened it, and
reached inside for his lunch. He pulled out a pair of shoes.
"Why is Dad feeding me shoes?" he asked.

"Hey!" Mike grabbed for the shoes. "That's my
bag!"

"Why is Dad feeding you shoes?" Ben asked.

"Ben, give it. I need those."

Ben held on to the shoes, noticing the writing on the
soles. He read out loud, "Robert E. Lee, Stonewall Jackson,
Appomattox Courthouse."

Mike grabbed the shoes and handed Ben another brown
bag from the table. This one contained Ben's lunch. "Heh-

heh.'' Mike laughed as he put the shoes back in the bag. "Those are my—buddies. I had 'em all sign my shoes for good luck!''

"You know somebody named William Tecumseh Sherman?'' Ben asked.

"Yeah,'' Mike said. "His locker's right next to mine.''

"And what about Appomattox Courthouse?'' Ben pressed.

"Tall guy?'' Mike answered "Captain of the basketball team?'' He grabbed the bag and ran out the door.

Ben nodded knowingly as he picked up his surprise lunch. He pushed away his breakfast plate with a frown and got ready to leave for school. "He's at it again,'' he said out loud to no one in particular.

Later that morning, Mike carefully made his way to history class wearing his special shoes. He entered just as the other students were settling into their seats. For the final few steps, he walked normally—he didn't want to attract attention. But he also didn't want to lose the precious information on the bottoms of his shoes.

As he sat down, Mike noticed the attractive girl in the next row looking curiously at his feet. "Karate,'' he said. "I just kicked over a brick wall.''

"Awesome!'' she said.

"It was nothing,'' Mike said, shrugging off the feat.

Boner slid into the seat next to Mike and started poring over his history text. "The one thing I know is that I don't know this,'' he said.

"Bone, my man,'' Mike said confidently, "you worry too much!''

"At least I'll have you for company in summer

school," Boner said. He flipped frantically through his history book.

"Not this time," Mike said. "I've got it aced!"

Boner looked shocked. "You're gonna tell me you studied this junk?"

"Oh, Boner, Boner, Boner," Mike said in a patronizing voice. "So young! So naive!"

Boner looked at Mike suspiciously. "You got cheat notes!" he said, suddenly realizing why Mike was so cool. "Hey, Eddie," Boner called out, pointing to Mike, "he's got ch—"

"Shhhh!" Mike said. "You say that too loud and people might get the wrong idea."

"Where are they?" Eddie asked, bolting to Mike's desk.

"I don't know what you're talking about," Mike said. "Go ahead. Search me. Full body. Strip search."

"No, thanks," Boner said, grimacing. Eddie had gone to stand lookout in the doorway.

Suddenly, Eddie whistled. "Teacher!" he alerted the class and dashed to his seat.

The class snapped to attention as Mr. DeWitt, a tired-looking man who often said he had seen it all in his years of teaching, trudged into the room. "All right, people," Mr. DeWitt called. He began handing out test sheets. "I trust you are all sufficiently frightened. If not, you should be, since this test will count for a quarter of your total grade."

"A quarter!" Boner whispered to Mike. "Yesterday he said it was only twenty-five percent!"

Mike sat still, looking straight ahead, keeping his cool.

"This is a multiple-choice test," Mr. DeWitt explained. "You have thirty minutes, and your papers will be graded before you leave. You may begin.'' He walked to his desk, and the students attacked their papers.

Mike looked around carefully to see if the coast was clear. Just as he was about to peek at his shoes, Mr. DeWitt walked nearby and stood by Mike's desk. Mike was forced to focus his eyes on the test paper. He looked at the sheet and mumbled to himself, ''The final northern battle of the Civil War was the (A) Battle of Bull Run, (B) Battle of Gettysburg, or (C) Battle of the Network Stars.''

Mike looked up at Mr. DeWitt, who gave a satisfied smile, pleased by his own sense of humor. Mike looked back at his paper and checked off an answer.

''Gettysburg,'' he said to himself. He checked off a few more answers and scanned the rest of the test. ''Hey!'' he said in a loud and surprised voice. ''I actually know this stuff!''

Boner, Mr. DeWitt, and the rest of the class laughed out loud.

''Okay, class, let's settle down. You have twenty-five minutes left to complete the test. That includes you, too, Mr. Seaver,'' he said, smiling at Mike.

''Yes, sir!'' Mike said. He zipped through the exam, practically jumping for joy because he knew the answers to the questions.

''Time's up,'' Mr. DeWitt called. ''Pass your papers forward.''

A buzz of activity filled the room as the students passed their papers to the front and whispered to each other about the test.

''While I correct these tests,'' Mr. DeWitt announced, ''I want you to begin reading the next chapter, starting on page two-oh-five.''

Twenty minutes later, Mr. DeWitt rose from his desk

and said, "Put your books away now, and I will return your exams." He walked slowly down the aisles handing back the corrected tests to the class. "Some of your tests results did surprise me," he said. He walked over to Boner's desk. "For instance," he said, reading Boner's test paper, "it was interesting to learn from Mr. Stabone that General Grant's first name was Lou."

Boner gulped as Mr. DeWitt placed the paper, facedown, on his desk. "I can't look! I can't look!" he said, putting his hand on his test. "I gotta look!" he cried out, turning over the paper. Eyeing the grade he laughed ecstatically. "Sixty-seven! All right!" he shouted.

Mike and the rest of the class broke into a round of applause.

"All right," Mr. DeWitt said, silencing them. "In what is perhaps the biggest shock I've sustained in my teaching career since boys started wearing earrings, the highest grade in the class, a ninety-four, was earned by— Mike Seaver!"

Mike and Boner broke out in cheers, and Mike jumped from his seat onto his desk doing a victory dance. "I am number one!" he chanted. "I am number one!"

"Mr. Seaver," the teacher called, motioning Mike to get off the desk. "Before we schedule a press conference, I have to ask. How does a student whose very name has become synonymous with the phrase *D-minus* manage such a grade?"

Mike sat triumphantly at his desk. "What can I say, Mr. DeWitt? When you got it, you got it?" He leaned back in his chair, clasped his hands behind his head, and propped his feet up on the desk.

Mr. DeWitt peered down at Mike's shoes. "And now," he said, seeing the history notes on the soles, "I see where you 'got it' from!''

Mike continued to smile, having completely forgotten about his notes. Then, suddenly, he remembered. Instinctively he pulled his feet off the desk in horror. He smiled weakly at Mr. DeWitt. At that moment the bell rang.

"Class dismissed," Mr. DeWitt called, as students began pushing back their chairs, piling up their books, and dashing for the door. "Mr. Seaver," he added, "you are not dismissed."

Mike gulped and slumped down in his chair. "I can't believe this is happening," he mumbled. "I finally learn something and now this!"

"So, now we have an answer to my question," Mr. DeWitt said as he gathered up the papers on his desk. "Don't we, Mr. Seaver?"

Mike jumped up from his seat and bolted to the front of the room. "You mean you're actually calling me a cheater?" he asked indignantly.

"Bingo!" Mr. DeWitt said, smiling grimly. "Give me your shoes."

"Okay," Mike said. "So a couple of things were written on my shoes."

"Mr. Seaver, don't try to fool Willy DeWitt! In my years here, I've seen cheat notes written on shirt sleeves, watchbands, fingernails, and once on a brassiere." He pointed to Mike's feet. "The shoes. Now!" Slowly, Mike removed his shoes and handed them to Mr. DeWitt. "But what'll I wear?" he asked.

"I don't know," the teacher said. "But you would have saved a lot of copying time if you had just made sandals out of the pages of your history book."

"But, Mr. DeWitt . . ." Mike implored.

Mr. DeWitt motioned for Mike to hand him the shoes.

Wearing only his socks, Mike stood before the teacher.

"Have your parent, guardian, or parole officer call for an appointment," Mr. DeWitt said as he held the shoes away from him, apparently beginning to smell them. "The sooner the better." He walked to the door, looked back at Mike, and went into the hall, leaving Mike alone in the room.

Angry, Mike kicked the teacher's desk, forgetting he wasn't wearing shoes. "Oww!!" he cried out.

Boner and Eddie walked into the room. "He beat you?" Boner asked, seeing Mike dancing on one foot in pain.

"No," Mike said, rubbing his toe. "He just took my shoes."

"That stinks, Mike," Eddie said.

"Yeah," Boner agreed, sniffing the air. "Real bad, too."

"What really bothers me is that he thinks I cheated," Mike said angrily.

Boner and Eddie looked at one another. "Boy," Boner said flatly, "hard to imagine."

"He wouldn't even take my word that I didn't!" Mike cried.

"Oh, yeah," Eddie said.

"Seaver," Boner said with a sly smile, "you really are good!"

"What does that mean?" Mike asked angrily.

Boner looked at him in surprise. "I mean, for a guy who faces suspension—and an F in history—you're cool enough to play innocent."

"But I am innocent!" Mike shouted.

"Wow! And outraged, too!" Boner said sarcastically. "Outraged, is tough," he said to Eddie.

"I can only work up to a small frenzy, myself," Eddie admitted.

Mike looked at his friends. "You guys don't believe me?" he asked incredulously.

Eddie and Boner looked at each other and cracked up in laughter. "Hey, Mikey. It's us," Eddie said, when he got his breath. "We know you!"

"Guys," Mike said seriously, "I didn't cheat!"

"No," Boner said. "You didn't look at those answers on your feet even once!" He and Eddie started laughing at Mike again.

"I'm not kidding around," Mike insisted.

Boner suddenly looked around the room, then pointed to a plant on Mr. DeWitt's desk. "Pssst, Eddie," he whispered. "DeWitt's probably got the room bugged, too!" He leaned forward toward the plant. "Of course, Mike," he said loudly. "You would never cheat!"

"Hey, I didn't cheat, and I don't like people assuming that I did! Got it?" Mike shouted. He turned and stormed out of the room.

Boner and Eddie watched Mike leave, his socks flapping as he walked. "Mike Seaver can't even spell the word *cheat*," Boner said in a loud voice, directly into the plant. In a softer voice, as they moved away from the desk, he said, "Mike's lucky he didn't have stuff written on his pants." They burst into laughter.

Later that afternoon, Carol was sprawled on the living room couch, watching television.

"Five nights this week," the announcer boomed, "the story that had all America reading, will have all America watching. At eighteen, she was a nun, at twenty-one, an acrobat, at thirty-seven, the mistress of a President. Joan Collins is . . .''

''Old,'' Carol said. She switched off the TV set. At the same time, the front door opened and Mike came in. ''Hi, Mike,'' she said.

''Hi.''

''What's the matter?'' she asked.

''How do you know something's the matter?'' he asked defiantly.

''Because you didn't say, 'Hi, Skunkbreath,' or 'hi, Nerdface,' or 'hi, Fido.' So what's the matter?''

Mike collapsed onto the couch beside her. ''Carol, I'm living a nightmare,'' he moaned. ''Nobody believes me. Not Boner, not Eddie, not Cheech, not Murray.''

''What are you talking about?'' she asked.

''Mr. DeWitt accused me of cheating on my history exam today,'' he said.

Carol sat bolt upright. ''You passed?''

''Yeah, I passed,'' Mike said. ''As a matter of fact, I got the highest grade in the class.''

Carol stared at her brother and burst out laughing.

''It was ninety-four,'' Mike said.

Carol laughed even harder, unable to speak.

''Is this your way of saying you don't believe me, either?'' he asked.

''Stop! Stop!'' Carol shrieked, bent over in hysterics.

''Fine. Don't believe me, skunkbreath, nerdface, Fido!''

Convulsed with laughter, Carol helplessly beat a sofa pillow.

Mike stormed out of the living room. As he pushed open the kitchen door, he found his parents putting away groceries. ''Mom, Dad, how great to see you!'' he oozed, causing his parents to eye each other suspiciously.

"Is he talking to us?" Maggie asked Jason.

"I just mean, knowing that I can count on you guys makes me feel happy," Mike said.

"The giddiness is contagious, Mike," his father said.

"You're welcome," Mike said. He crossed over to the refrigerator and opened the door.

His parents traded glances. "Do you have a fever?" his mother asked. She walked over and felt Mike's forehead.

"Mom!"

"Say, Maggie," Jason said. "You don't suppose this has anything to do with Mike's history test, do you?"

Mike put down the container of milk he was holding. "Well, you know, I'm darn glad you brought that up!" he said.

"I'd better sit down," his mother said and slid into a chair.

"What happened?" his father asked.

"Well, there's not too much to be said about the test itself," Mike said.

"Say it, anyway," his father demanded.

Mike shrugged. "I passed."

"Completely?" his mother asked in surprise.

"Yes," Mike said.

"All right, Mike!" his father said, slapping him on the back.

"I knew you could do it!" his mother added, jumping up and hugging Mike. "Congratulations!"

"What did I tell you? I knew that studying would pay off," his father said.

"Thank you," Mike said. "But I have some bad news, too. Dad, you'd better sit for this."

"Just say what it is, Mike," his father said.

"Jason, I have a feeling you should sit," Maggie insisted, returning to her seat.

Jason sat down.

Mike walked to the center of the kitchen. "What I am about to tell you," he said, "will get you both quite angry. You will be outraged at the shoddy treatment I have received from Mr. DeWitt. I want your word that you won't go off half-cocked and try to get him fired or something."

Jason eyed his son suspiciously. "I promise to be fully cocked, Mike," he said. "Get on with it."

"Good. Okay then, Mr. DeWitt accused me of . . ." Mike lowered his voice to a whisper and added, "cheating." In a louder voice he said, "Now just calm down!"

"I'm in control," his father said flatly. Maggie remained silent.

"I didn't cheat!" Mike cried out.

"Then why would Mr. DeWitt think you did?" his mother asked.

"You know," Mike said, "I've been asking myself that question all afternoon."

"And what answer did you come up with?" his father asked.

"I, ah, guess he didn't, expect me to do too well on the test," Mike suggested.

"Well?" his mother asked. "You did well?" She turned to Jason. "He did well. How well?" she asked, turning back to Mike.

"I rarely pay attention to grades," Mike said casually.

"What did you get?" his father demanded. "Seventy?"

"Uh, no," Mike said.

"Seventy-five?" his mother asked with alarm.

"Well . . ."

"Eighty?" she pressed, her frenzy building.

"See . . ." Mike started to say.

"Eight-five?" his mother almost shouted.

"Actually . . ." Mike said.

"Ninety?" she shrieked, jumping up from her seat.

"Four . . ." Mike added.

"Ninety-four?" his mother repeated. "Why, Michael Seaver. I'm ashamed of you! How could you cheat!"

"I swear to you I did not cheat!"

"Hold on here a minute," his father said, still digesting the numbers. "Is this ninety-four out of one hundred?"

"Dad," Mike said, "I swear to you I did not cheat. I give you my word of honor."

"I believe you," his father said instantly. Maggie and Mike both looked at him. "Really?" they said in unison.

"If my son is giving me his word, I've got to believe him," he said.

Maggie considered this and sat down again at the table. "You're right," she agreed. "I believe you, too, Mike."

"Believe what?" Ben asked as he entered the kitchen. No one answered him.

"All right!" Mike said and heaved a sigh of relief. "I knew I could count on you guys. I'm so sorry for every miserable thing I've ever done to make your world a living hell."

"Well," his mother said, pulling him to her in a hug, "I'm sorry I doubted you, Mike. But it's a tough story to believe if you put yourself in my shoes."

Ben giggled. "Mom's shoes aren't big enough for all the answers," he said.

Jason and Maggie looked at him with confused expressions.

"Right," Mike said. "The shoes. Thanks, Benny.

How could I have forgotten to tell you guys the funniest part? You're just going to love this!''

"There you are," Maggie said to Jason as she stepped onto the front porch. "You're going to freeze out here."

"No," he said bitterly. "I've got my angst to keep me warm."

Maggie shivered in the cold night air. "Could you share some with me?" She smiled. Jason put his arm around her but his mood was still remote. "Jason," she said. "I have something to tell you. I didn't want to tell you, but since you're blaming yourself for what Mike did, I figure you need some good news."

Jason looked down at her.

"You're not really Mike's father," she said, trying to sound believable. Jason smiled. "There. That's better." Maggie hugged him to her.

"You know what I've been thinking about?" Jason asked.

"That when Mike looked you in the eye and lied, it made you question your whole approach to teaching our kids the value of truth and honesty," Maggie said. "You've been wondering if, instead of encouraging them by example, a little fear of punishment might have been more effective. You're probably remembering the time when Mike was eight and he lied about finger-painting the new rug. I wanted to spank him, and you convinced me that reasoning with him was better."

Jason smiled again. "How did you do that?" he asked. "That's exactly right!"

"It's not that amazing. I'll bet you know what I'm thinking right now."

Jason looked into Maggie's eyes. "You're thinking,"

he said, "that no matter how disappointed we both are in Mike, we still love him dearly. That we'll do our best to mold him into an honest man. And even if we fail, he can have a very productive life in politics," Jason concluded.

"I would have said used-car sales, but it's the same idea," Maggie said.

Jason tightened his arm around her, and they stood watching their breath forming clouds of smoke.

"Mom! Dad!" Carol's cry broke the silence. She stuck her head out the front door. "I want to watch this show about famous artists who have cut off parts of their bodies, and Ben keeps changing the channel back to this dumb movie called, *Father of a Teenage Hooligan*!

"Carol, I'm going with Ben this time," her father said. Turning to Maggie, he added, "Let's go and watch. I might learn something."

Later that night, Mike lay on his bed, tossing his books one by one at the basketball hoop on the wall. Systematically, he threw a book then reached for a handful of chips from a bag on his bed.

"Mike?" Ben called, after knocking on the door and getting no answer.

"Benedict Arnold!" Mike shouted.

"No. Ben Seaver," he said.

"Get away!" Mike shouted.

Ben opened the door slowly and walked into Mike's room. He was carrying a piece of chicken in a napkin. "Want some dinner?" he asked, handing Mike the napkin.

"No," Mike said. He reached for a potato chip. "I am no longer eating any food that is paid for by people who think I'm a liar."

"Then what are those?" Ben asked, pointing to the potato chips.

Mike shrugged. "I'm easing into it," he explained. "What do you want, anyway?"

"Mike, I didn't mean to get you in such big trouble," Ben apologized.

Mike considered Ben's answer for a moment. "Yeah, well, I knew the shoes would be too much for them," he admitted, accepting Ben's apology. "It's been like that all day. Everybody at school, even Boner. And last year I actually convinced him I was an alien!" Mike paused for a moment and looked over at his brother. "Ben, people are acting like they expect me to cheat—like I'm that kind of low scuzzball. I admit I had planned to cheat, but when I looked at the test I knew the answers. I guess dad was right—studying helps!"

"I believe you," Ben said firmly.

"What?" Mike asked. "What do you believe?"

"I mean," Ben said, "I believe whatever you say. Whether it's the truth or not."

Mike smiled. "I'll tell you something weird," he said, starting to eat the chicken from the napkin without even realizing it. "When Mom and Dad did believe me, everything was okay." He swallowed a bite of chicken. "My gosh!" he said incredulously. "I actually care what they think about me!"

"I care what they think about me," Ben said.

"Sure. You're nine. It's okay to feel that way at nine," Mike explained.

"That's good," Ben said.

"But I'm fifteen. I'm supposed to think my parents are scum."

"Are you sure?" Ben asked.

"Yeah. Everybody knows that. It's on TV all the time," Mike said.

Ben thought for a moment. "I guess you're not normal, then," he said.

"I never wanted to be," Mike admitted. "But I never thought it would turn out like this."

"I'm sorry," Ben said.

"I'm shocked," Mike confessed. "And if you ever tell anyone about this, you'll be able to eat through the top of your head."

"I believe you," Ben said.

"Thanks kid." Mike smiled.

"Mike, Mr. DeWitt will go a lot easier with you if you just admit what you did," his mother advised as they waited in the classroom for the teacher the following afternoon.

"I don't care," Mike insisted.

"Well, we do, Mike," his father said. "Will you at least pretend to care about what we think?"

"Sure," Mike said reluctantly. "But no one is going to believe me."

"Why should anyone?" his father asked.

"Because I didn't . . ." Mike said automatically, stopping midsentence in defeat. "It doesn't matter."

"Should we have believed you in the seventh grade when you told us that the D on your report card meant 'darn good'?" his father asked.

"That was three years ago," Mike pointed out.

"What about in the eighth grade, when you told the school your name was Seaverman so you could take all the Jewish holidays off?" his mother recalled.

"And just this week . . ." his father started to say.

"All right, all right. Sometimes . . . I lie. But there's a big difference between being a liar and being a LIAR. I mean, you're supposed to know when I'm telling the truth. What kind of parents are you anyway?"

"Disappointed," his father said.

"You want to know the truth?" Mike shouted. "Okay, I'll tell you the truth. Yeah, I was GOING to cheat. I figured it was the only way. So the night before the test I was up half the night, copying all that stuff on my shoes because I had to pass that test. But somehow it didn't go just on my shoes, it got in my head. Sure blew ME away! Anyway, when it came time to look for the answers, I didn't have to. I KNEW them!" Mike turned away, his eyes filling with tears. His parents looked at one another.

"I'd like to believe you, Mike," his mother said.

"Yeah, sure," Mike said sarcastically.

"Mike, you're not exactly the kind of guy who has a reputation for knowing things like . . . Abraham Lincoln was the seventeenth president," his father pointed out.

"Yeah," Mike said, then added, "the sixteenth president."

"Right," his father said, "Grant was the seventeenth."

"Grant was the eighteenth," Mike corrected. "Andrew Johnson was the seventeenth. He became president when Lincoln was assassinated on April 14, 1865."

Jason and Maggie looked at Mike in amazement, suddenly realizing the truth.

Mr. DeWitt entered the classroom. "Dr. and Mrs. Seaver," he said, "I'm Willis DeWitt. Glad you could come. Should we get right down to business?"

Jason and Maggie stood together facing the teacher.

"Absolutely, Mr. DeWitt," Jason said. "Mike did not

cheat on that test, and it's important that we clear this up.''

Maggie and Jason put their arms around Mike and stared at Mr. DeWitt.

''And it would have been so easy for him to do,'' Maggie said, ''what with all the answers written on the bottoms of his shoes.''

Mr. DeWitt stared at the trio as though they were crazy. ''Yes,'' he said, shaking his head. ''I'd say so.''

''Mike has explained the entire situation to us,'' Maggie said. ''The evidence is against him, but we're convinced he's telling the truth about not cheating on the test.''

''But, Mrs. Seaver,'' the teacher said. ''The shoes . . .?''

''The shoes could be considered a learning tool, Mr. DeWitt,'' Jason said. ''Instead of taking notes in a composition book, Mike used shoes. His intentions were not the best, and for that he'll be punished. But his performance on the test was based on his actual knowledge, not on what was written on the shoes.''

''Well,'' Mr. DeWitt said, rubbing his chin. ''Perhaps the best way to clear this up is to give him another test right away. If you will wait here, Dr. and Mrs. Seaver, I will prepare a new test which Mike can take in one hour.''

''That would be more than fair, Mr. DeWitt,'' Jason said. ''We'll be here.''

An hour later, Mr. DeWitt returned to the classroom where Mike and his parents waited. He handed a test paper to Mike.

''Thank you for letting him take this make-up test, Mr. DeWitt,'' Jason said.

''No problem,'' he said.

''I think Mike knows now that intending to cheat is just as bad as cheating itself,'' Jason added.

''That's what my ex-wife said in court,'' Mr. DeWitt

noted wryly.

"Shhh," Maggie said. "He's trying to take a test."

Mr. DeWitt and the Seavers turned toward the center of the classroom where Mike was seated at a desk, concentrating on the test.

He had stripped down to a basketball tank top and gym shorts, and he wore no shoes.

As they were watching him, Mike suddenly reached down to scratch his foot.

"Ah-ah-ah!" Mr. DeWitt called to him.

"Itch," Mike explained, turning his attention back to the exam sheet.

"Another long day." Maggie sighed, and snuggled into the living room couch. "I feel like I've been through the mill!"

"Me, too," Jason said. "But at least we got things straightened out with Mike. In spite of it all, I think he learned an important lesson."

"I hope so," Maggie said. "I never want to go through THAT again! He was a sight in those gym clothes though, wasn't he?" She giggled as she leafed through the *TV GUIDE*.

"What's on the tube tonight?" Jason asked. "I could use a good relaxing evening of TV."

"It's the fifth night of that Joan Collins miniseries," Maggie said.

"That might be interesting," Jason said.

Maggie read from the *TV Guide*; " 'Tonight Joan leaves the Pope to marry a bricklayer.' "

"OOOOooo," Jason sighed. "Mike won't want to miss this one!"

"Where is Mike, anyway?" Maggie asked. "I haven't

seen him since dinner.''

"Studying for his French test tomorrow," Jason said.

"Do you really think he's serious about studying, now?" Maggie asked Jason as the sound of dull bass music began pounding overhead.

"I'd bet on it," Jason said, dusting the falling plaster from his hair. "Besides there's a new French girl in his class, and from what Mike tells me, she's worth studying for!"